THE HAMMERFIELD PAYOFF

THE SCIENCE OFFICER: VOLUME 8

BLAZE WARD

KNOTTED ROAD PRESS

The Hammerfield Payoff
Volume 8
Blaze Ward
Copyright © 2017 Blaze Ward
All rights reserved
Published by Knotted Road Press
www.KnottedRoadPress.com

ISBN: 978-1-943663-65-1

Cover art:
Copyright © Luca Oleastri - Dreamstime.com | Spaceship and navigation interface

Cover and interior design copyright © 2017 Knotted Road Press

Never miss a release!
If you'd like to be notified of new releases, sign up for my newsletter.

I only send out newsletters once a quarter, will never spam you, or use your email for nefarious purposes. You can also unsubscribe at any time.

http://www.blazeward.com/newsletter/

Demigod

Greater Than The Gods Intended

Other Science Fiction Stories

Myrmirdons

Moonshot

Menelaus

Earthquake Gun

Moscow Gold

Fairchild

White Crane

***The Collective* Universe**

The Shipwrecked Mermaid

Imposters

BOOK TWENTY-FOUR:
ALKONOST

Javier studied the big bridge of the transport he was in the process of hijacking.

Metal walls painted white, instead of the expensive wood paneling that that punk Slavkov had used in all the party spaces elsewhere. Similar floors with a rough enough tread that Javier's usual soft moccasins would have been uncomfortable, thus the heavy boots. Hell, even the air had a stale, dry taste to it that told him the humidifiers needed to be tuned. Something for Ilan to do when he got here.

In front of him, Javier watched the night through a transparent window that was three meters tall and nine wide, overlooking the bow of the giant vessel. The night sky was finally turning to complete black as the sun set.

Javier would have left the wall as a reinforced bulkhead and hung a viewscreen on it, if it were up to him. Slavkov must like his view organic rather than electronic. Javier had them leave the blast screen down for now.

He turned back to the rest of the room.

Captain's station at the back of a diamond-layout facing him. Three crew stations. Ramps curving up both sides of the bridge behind that to an overlook two meters up. The space below the platform was a well-designed rest room, so nobody had to be far off the bridge when on duty.

Another deck up, and the designer had put in a mezzanine with three big levels like a flat ziggurat, up two stairs to the next step, twice. That was where the party would be, both during re-entry, and whenever the owner was aboard.

Two hours had passed since Javier had very quietly raised the black flag, but he was still wearing what he thought of as the cruise ship uniform he had taken from a crew member who was now a prisoner downstairs. They were waiting their turn to orbit.

Valko Slavkov, villain extraordinaire and owner of this vessel, had just now gotten up to the edge of the atmosphere in his own personal shuttle, a private cruise ship for him and a few close friends and a couple hundred fawning servants. In another hour or so, the man would make his first jump, bouncing clear out of the system on the way to a party somewhere, leaving behind *The Land Leviathan*, a ten-car tracked vehicle that doubled as a mobile resort on the desert worlds he liked.

He was probably already planning to meet up with it again in a few months, on some other planet.

Down on the ground, Javier smiled. With all the bimbos and cooks removed and departed with Slavkov, the entire remaining engineering crew of the Leviathan was only eighteen people. Plus another dozen to fly the nameless transport.

Djamila Sykora, Dragoon of the First-Rate-Galleon-turned-pirate *Hammerfield*, probably couldn't have taken them all by herself.

Probably.

Fortunately, Javier hadn't just brought her, but also her six gun-bunnies, two pathfinders, and three other recently-recruited assassins. And one extra engineer in Afia Burakgazi, but Afia was here to help him, not Djamila.

The drivers and engineers on the Land Leviathan had put up no fuss whatsoever when the killers had stepped out from cover just as the crew finished locking down the giant train for transport. At that point they were just looking forward to a cold drink. Javier had even locked them away in their cabins and left them with a couple cases of beer, just to keep them out of trouble.

He wasn't here for their souls.

If they behaved.

No, identifying himself as Captain Navarre and promising to let them go when he was done had been a magic wand.

Reputations are wonderful things, when people know you'll kill them at the first hint of trouble. And politely drop them at their own doorstep if they are good.

A number of Slavkov's people could testify to that. And Abraam Tamaz's memory would keep the rest in line. Still, he would have rather been somewhere else.

Javier finished his train of thought with a sigh and fixed his attention on the ship's former captain, standing off to one side with Sykora close enough to growl at the man.

She liked doing that.

"One down," Javier said to the man in a deliberately cheerful voice. "I'll remind you that my cruiser is out there watching, and will be all set to jump in and help if something happens. Her orders are to annihilate the two escorts in orbit at the slightest provocation, and I have no doubts she'll carry them out with gusto."

The man blanched and swallowed. Up until now, everything had been a bluff, as far as the man knew, but he was also aware that his head was first on the chopping block if Javier took a mind to it.

"What's the next sequence?" Javier continued.

Afia was seated in the main piloting station, all big, brown eyes that only looked innocent as she watched.

"I'll send a signal to the two gunships: Escort Red and Escort Blue," the captain replied. "Then we lift on autopilot, as always, and rendezvous with them in high orbit before we break out and move to the first safe jump distance. All three ships match telemetry and we jump to the next destination, in this case, on the path to *Nidavellir*. The Leviathan is scheduled for a major maintenance cycle."

"Yes," Javier nodded with a grim smile. "Joyous *Nidavellir*, corporate home to Walvisbaai Industrial. A hellhole so corrupt that it makes *Meehu Platform* look reputable by comparison. Safe for traveling virgins, as it were."

Rather than answer, the man shrugged. It wasn't his ship, he just commanded it. Valko Slavkov made those decisions.

And had chosen to hire Walvisbaai Industrial to kill Captain Navarre and the crew of the then-private-service Strike Corvette *Storm Gauntlet*, captained by one Zakhar Sokolov.

All in the name of petty pique.

Because Slavkov had hired Captain Navarre to steal something, expecting that the mercenary would unleash a bloody slaughter on a bunch of innocent-if-very-wealthy tourists in the process.

And those yahoos at Walvisbaai would have succeeded later at *Svalbard*, if not for Javier's sneakiness, Djamila's brutal efficiency, and Sokolov's deft ship-handling.

In failure, they had forced Javier's hand.

Storm Gauntlet was too damaged to continue this quest, this *War of the Pirate Clans*, so he enlisted his own slave master, his comrade-in-arms from the *Bryce* Navy, as a partner, and went off and stole the derelict last flagship of the *Neu Berne* fleet from her final resting place.

With her final crew still aboard.

He would have to return the bodies home, when this was done.

If he survived.

Or Suvi could do it, since she was now the *Sentience-In-Residence* aboard *Hammerfield*, flying these days as the private transport/warship publicly known as *Excalibur*. If something happened to him, she would handle the honors, after burning Walvisbaai and Slavkov to slag.

Javier let an angry smile take over his face.

He turned to Afia.

"Open a comm channel and stand by for liftoff," he said in a grim tone.

Javier hadn't chosen this war. He had just chosen to make them regret starting it, for however much longer they lived.

SUVI WAS SWIMMING in deep space like the galaxy's biggest reef shark. Long and gray and sleek and deadly, down in the deeper water where nobody could see her, just waiting to leap up and bite someone. She dug out her piano and added some ominous music as a background, while she completed her survey of the *Alkonost* system, most recent excursion destination for the cruising, tracked turtle known as the Land Leviathan.

The task kept her sharp, cataloging everything in the system, natural or man-made. She did it in every system she visited. In the old days, she and Javier would upload it to the folks in the *Concord* fleet responsible for keeping the *Gazeteer* up to date, slowly adding new systems, and old, forgotten ones, to the charts.

Suvi wasn't sure if they would keep up the habit, going forward, but she was prepared.

Alkonost was mostly boring. *VII* didn't even have an official name, but the very few locals called it *Gobi* for the tremendous steppes and arid wastelands that covered so much of the surface. One man apparently owned the entire star system, like some feudal monarch from old earth.

Whatever.

Suvi had watched impatiently as the first ship lifted off from the planet then idled merrily to the edge of the gravity well, only to vanish like a soap bubble, leaving a double handful of others in orbit, and a couple of stations.

That was probably good, because if something had gone wrong on the planet below, they either wouldn't have left, or would have gone like cats with their tails on fire.

But she only really cared about the two armed torpedo boats that remained behind now.

Hammerfield could overwhelm both of them with half her turrets tied behind her back, but this was supposed to be a sneak job.

Hide out beyond the range that most ships could actively track her, while her probe-cutter-grade sensors could read their manufacturer plates from here. Be an insurance policy in case Javier needed heads cracked together.

"Suvi," Piet Alferdinck called in a quiet voice. "What's our status, please?"

Rather than sit up in the big throne that was the captain's seat, Piet preferred the navigator's console. Even though he was in overall command right now, and acting more and more as the crew's executive officer.

Captain Sokolov's First Mate.

"The transport is deep in their lift, sir," she replied. "Orbital pulse will end in thirty-eight minutes and then the ship will insert into high orbit with targets Able and Baker."

Suvi had been afraid that she would chase Piet off.

He had been the *Pilot*, back on *Storm Gauntlet*. Looking at the logs, she was amazed at how good the man was at his task, a job that married skill with art. But he was a quiet man, and the *Concord* navy had a tendency to promote extroverts, not music history experts.

With her handling all the flying and navigating tasks, and able to do it orders of magnitude faster and more accurately than a human, this ship didn't need a dedicated pilot.

But they had bonded over music. And that was good.

These days, his boards didn't actually command the engines and gyros. Piet offered suggestions and improvements that she executed. And he had gotten even better, which was kinda amazing, until he told her that the key to that was that he didn't have to track systems for stability, so he could plan several moves ahead, trusting her to do the accounting and housekeeping.

Like Javier trusted her to handle things. It made a girl all tingly in the right places.

"Permission to soundtrack?" she asked.

Piet looked down at the spot on his board where her image appeared. Suvi was baseline today on crew screens: a tall, Finnish blond in a modified Concord yeoman's uniform. She hadn't even added extra arms or anything.

"What did you have in mind?" Piet replied with a smile in his eyes.

It was his bridge, after all, at least until Captain Sokolov came on duty. But the captain didn't really appreciate music.

"Something Thirtieth Century," Suvi replied. "From the *Utafiti mkubwa* period. The Great Exploring."

He raised an eyebrow at her.

"Granted," he said. "But quiet."

Suvi nodded. She hadn't actually forgotten about the other three crew members on the enormously oversized bridge, but she hadn't really been paying attention to them either, between the survey work and the shark fantasies.

She started with the overture to Olivier Janguo, the compressed, musical life story of the man who had gotten most of the credit for inventing the future, the device that would be known to history as the *Mchunguzi Systems Mark I.*

The first commercial stardrive capable of punching a starship through hyperspace.

Everything since then had been bigger and better models, but the basic theory of the physics had not changed much in the forty-six centuries since. Pick a direction, jump as far as you could, land, figure out where you were.

It was kinda like throwing a baseball. If you were good, you could nail the runner from right field, trying to make it home.

If you were a *Sentience*, you could calculate directions and probability arcs 20,000 times faster than a human could. Right now, that was useful, because she had a course laid in that would drop her well inside the planet's safe gravity zone, dangerously close to the planet, but right between the two escorts where she could split her turrets evenly and destroy them before they had a chance to notice.

If she had to.

Javier had always been a 'live and let live' kind of guy. She like that part.

Olivier Janguo had been a man for pure science, but he reportedly had recognized the stardrive for what it was: the ability to go off and be yourself without answering to anyone else, anywhere. His musical score, then, was grand and bold. Seeking what might be out there, in the era before humans conclusively proved that Fermi was right.

That there was nobody around but the humans. And their children.

Suvi let the music build slowly. It always brought her hope, those opening notes where the brass started off quietly, bringing in the woodwinds and strings slowly as a backdrop for the first big blast of sound as the galaxy was suddenly broken open.

Okay, so maybe she was over-analyzing the composer. A bit. Whatever.

Music made her smile. Today, it made the four people on the bridge smile, too. Hopefully, they would have nothing to do today but sit and monitor systems and communications.

Because if something went wrong, she wasn't going to ask for permission. Just move and shoot.

She would explain to Piet what had happened, after everything was done. Sitting over the corpses of the two dead escorts with a smoking blaster in her hand.

PART THREE

DJAMILA SYKORA WATCHED the scene unfold with something akin to pleasure.

It was a new feeling, enjoying life.

She considered experiencing some guilt over the whole concept, but decided it could wait. She had lived her whole thirty-eight years rebelling against the concept that she wasn't better than anyone else at a task she had identified for herself.

Perfectionism had taken her many places. Not all of them bright and cheery.

But she was trying to become someone else, now.

Someone who could experience simple pleasures in life, rather than keeping a running scorecard of all the things she should be doing to improve her current high mark next time.

Djamila supposed she should blame Javier, eventually. Even if he wasn't sure why. Without him, Djamila would have never met Suvi. Without Suvi, Afia Burakgazi would have never worked up the courage to upend Djamila's life.

Without Afia, no Zakhar.

Djamila felt herself blush, fought it, decided to accept her own internal reprobation. Zakhar Sokolov had been everything she had ever hoped for. And still the stern taskmaster captain who drove his crew to their own heights of excellence.

Djamila remembered to breathe out silently, so nobody heard her contented sigh.

Her job today was less security and more intimidation. She was almost a caryatid, a stone column carved into the shape of a woman that would come alive at the first hint of danger and fight.

Certainly, the transport's former captain, a slightly-squishy man named Berto Haaken, wasn't a threat to anyone. She had only heard stories and rumors about the man they were after, Valko Slavkov, but she had met half a hundred of the men he had hired for various tasks.

All of them had reminded her of the sorts of people you got when you cut corners and paid less than the going rate. You ended up with third-rate punks, but they were the desperate dregs of a galaxy with lots of people, too many guns and not enough opportunities to keep them out of trouble.

Armed mobs were useful, until you ran into professional killers, like Dragoon Sykora and her Combat Operations Team. Or the assassins she had added for this mission.

Captain Haaken waited patiently on what had been his bridge. Javier asked the occasional question. Or, more frequently, Afia did.

This was not a combat warship. It was a cargo transport, purpose-built to haul the biggest land vessel Djamila had ever seen. It had to be wasteful of space, because there was so much needed, and no use for it.

The Land Leviathan was comprised of ten, tracked cars, like a train or articulated truck. Each car was sixty meters square front and side, and thirty tall. The whole beast was nearly seven hundred meters long at rest, as it was now. Carefully parked in the bay that made up the bulk of this transport, wrapped around it like a horseshoe.

And this whole vessel existed just to haul the Leviathan between worlds when Slavkov got bored with one and moved on to the next.

Djamila was not impressed.

She understood wealth, having seen a number of people

either born to it or having had it thrust upon them. Few were as petty and childish as Slavkov.

Fewer still had chosen to start wars with men like Zakhar Sokolov and Javier Aritza.

"What are they up to, Afia?" Javier asked the engineer who was overseeing the piloting station.

As automated as this ship was, Djamila might have flown them to orbit, but none of them could have even guessed that ahead of time. Plus, they had needed Afia's skill with locks and systems to get this far.

"All guns unlocked and just waiting for someone like *Storm Gauntlet* to appear for an ass-kicking session," the tiny woman replied in a laconic tone completely at odds with the focus she had on the various screens.

Djamila approved of both the tone and the professionalism. Hopefully, some of it would rub off on Javier, eventually.

She didn't have a great deal of faith in the concept, but even the horse in the fable might learn to sing.

"Anything aimed at us?" Javier replied.

"Negative," Afia smiled. "We're the harmless, old lady they have to help walk across the street. Eighteen minutes until the next communications check-in."

Djamila wasn't keyed up for combat, but she retained a professional paranoia, especially on someone else's stolen starship, so she was not surprised when Javier rounded on Captain Haaken and rotated from charming to intense.

"I presume you will call them personally, in your guise as commodore," Javier said in a voice suddenly harsher. "And order them to fall into line or something?"

Djamila was close enough to smell the sudden flop sweat break out on the ma:, a rank, vinegary taste in her mouth. She hoped Javier didn't cause the man to wet himself in fear.

"Uhm, well, you see…" the man stammered in response.

"Yes or no?" Javier override him. He pointed at Afia. "She's probably good enough to locate what I need in your logs. Maybe even good enough to play it back for them now. Sixteen minutes."

Javier had a way of knocking people off balance verbally. She couldn't mimic it, but Djamila had watched it enough to have a feel for it. Dropping the other shoe by counting down an invisible clock. As effective as it was distracting.

"Yes, sir. I mean no, sir," Haaken snapped to. "That is, one of my men would transmit the next jump vector under my orders, but I wouldn't speak to those two captains unless something went wrong."

"Good enough," Javier relented and smiled at the man.

Djamila watched the captain shiver unconsciously. Not a man used to being confronted with violence, even if she was the only one here openly armed.

Haaken probably wasn't used to a dangerous woman, either. He looked like the type that was at Temple every nine-day, loudly singing the hymns and pretending to be just another bourgeois peon.

Those were usually the weirdest, once you peeled away the public layers, but she didn't say anything.

Javier pulled a small package from his pocket and handed it to the engineer.

"I'm pretty sure the standard vector coordinates for *Nidavellir* are already loaded," he said with a wintry smile. "Transmit those to the escorts when we get there, and use the vector on this chip instead."

"Where are you taking us?" Captain Haaken stuttered nervously again.

"I'm taking you and your crew to a nice resort for an all-expenses-paid two-week stay," Javier smiled. "And then I'm taking the Leviathan on to *Nidavellir*, like you planned."

Captain Haaken shivered some more at the tone.

Even Djamila was uncomfortable with Aritza's solution to the problem of a pirate war, but she had to admit it would probably be effective.

Hopefully, the rest of the galaxy would survive.

PART FOUR

Yên reviewed the file once again, as if the words on the screen would suddenly rearrange themselves into a new pattern. One that made sense. Creator knew, nothing else did.

He rubbed his eyes and put his elbows up on the desk. It was late. He was close to halfway through what would normally be his sleep shift, but the file had come by Fleet Courier, and he needed time to digest it. So he was up too late.

Yên rose from the desk in his little office, a room barely bigger than his outstretched arms, and twisted his back each way to loosen up the kinks. The gray walls in here were soothing, as was the green/brown carpet, but it wasn't going to make him any less tired.

He moved to the porthole and stared out at the forever-night sky. He supposed he could lean far enough to see *Merankorr* below him, if he wanted. Or bring up a small telescope and spot some of the other orbital stations and ships sharing the sky with him.

But right now, he just wanted to be alone. To think.

To wonder how they had gotten here.

Concord Captain Nguyên Ayokunle studied his faint reflection in the glass. For a fifty-five-year-old man, he was still skinny and unbowed, even if the dark skin of his face was starting to get serious about pruning up. And the fluffy ringlets of his hair had gone totally white.

Probably why his friend shaved his head.

Yên thought about the man he had met here, his old friend…

No, think of him as Zakhar Sokolov. That's who he has made himself into. Do not out him to anyone without a very good reason.

Had it really been forty years since they'd met at Freshman Orientation?

The computer screen mocked him when he turned back around. But one did not ignore a message from the Naval Estimates Board, even couched in polite terms.

NEB was the *Concord's Fleet's* intelligence arm. The spies. The analysts. The assassins.

After all, as Commodore, Senior Captain of the fleet's permanent civilian-related installations at *Merankorr*, it had been his report that started all this.

The chance recognition of a man he originally knew by another name, once upon a time, now linked to that of an organization that the *Concord* would have broken, had they jurisdiction or reach. A man who might politely be referred to as a pirate. Up until now, a ghost with no history, no connection to anything, until one day several years ago, when he appeared on their scanners flying a small, de-commissioned warship, but never doing anything that gave the *Concord* a reason to pursue him.

There weren't enough ships, or men, or resources, to chase all of them.

Yên snorted. There was barely enough anything: men, ships, or money; to hold the frontiers against the barbarians, let alone go out into the darkness and chase them as they fled.

He had always been a history nut. The fall of Athens. The fall of Rome. The fall of Byzantium. The fall of Spain. Et cetera. Et cetera. Et cetera.

He didn't think the *Concord* was going down. These days always felt more like the squishy period after a war, when everyone demobilized their armies and navies, then muddled through the inevitable recessions and depressions that resulted from too many workers and not enough work.

You got revolutionary fervor spilling over. And criminals.

And a man you hadn't spoken with in seventeen years suddenly showing up as a pirate. Commanding a warship big enough, and dangerous enough, that the spooks back home had gotten involved.

Yên moved back around to read the tail end of the message.

You will immediately travel to the Binhai *system on official business and make contact with the* Khatum of Altai, *owner of the vessel* Shangdu. *Reports place the aforementioned vessel,* Excalibur, *in the company of the* Khatum, *who is assumed to be a part-owner based on your own reports.*

You will determine the current location of the vessel, Excalibur, *and her intentions.*

While ongoing strife between such organizations as the Jarre Foundation and Walvisbaai Industrial is to be commended, it must not be allowed to endanger galactic shipping or Concord *interests. You will identify the immediate risks and suggest a course of action to mitigate them.*

At least they were letting him handle this, and not assigning some random flunky to the task. He knew the man, this pirate captain named Sokolov who had been somebody else once. And official business meant whatever transport he could hire, since there were no *Concord* warships handy that he could flag down for a ride.

At least not yet.

The *Merankorr* squadron did have a Class II Warmaster available he could call on. That would be enough to take on a First-Rate-Galleon.

Yên hoped he wouldn't end up having to kill his oldest friend in the galaxy.

BOOK TWENTY-FIVE: BINHAI

PART ONE

BEHNAM LOOKED up with a critical eye at the interruption to her salad.

She had chosen to eat lunch today in the public spaces, rather than back in her personal quarters. It was early enough according to the local clock that guests staying up too late would have completed a leisurely brunch and gone off to do whatever they did in the hours of artificial daylight. Probably out for a swim in the lake that sat at the center of her starship.

How often did you find an artificial lake on a starship? Pools? Certainly, but an ellipse two kilometers long by one wide? With an island in the center that exceeded twenty-two thousand square meters?

Luxury. Decadence.

And extremely profitable.

Not that she needed money. She was the *Khatum of Altai,* and already one of the richest women in space. But she was also a businesswoman, and running a highly profitable resort in the shape of a giant starship made her people that much happier when it helped lower their taxes.

And kept her off-planet for long stretches of time. Enjoying herself.

But business was apparently intent on intruding today.

She had chosen this alcove because it was just public enough to be seen, while at the same time private enough that nobody would bother her. Several plants in pots obscured the sand-colored walls and rails. And a pair of guards one man and one woman, and a single step up, made sure that anyone bothering this woman's lunch would not be an idle decision.

Which is probably why someone had escalated something to Tömörbaatar. And he had chosen to come see her in person, instead of just sending her a quick message.

The *Iron Hero of Altai* was her Provost, as far as those things went. Head of the traveling household, rather than the government back home, although those people were smart enough to answer to him, as well.

Behnam set the large bowl of leafy greens down and slid her fork into it. The wooden table clunked and the metal rang.

Tömörbaatar was dressed sedately today. Black robes embroidered in blue and red and his head topped with the ever-present cute little box cap in white silk that he had adopted as a uniform.

She did not feel like treating this as an emergency situation, so she gestured for him to join her. As Tömörbaatar sat, she refilled her glass with cool water and poured one for him, trying to gauge the significance of his calling upon her.

A true emergency would have caused a larger ruckus somewhere. Less would have been sufficiently covered with a quick ping.

The last time he had come to find her had been when Captain Navarre had returned.

She smiled at that memory, catapulted back to both times she had been with the man.

At forty-nine, Behnam worked assiduously to maintain her health and shape. Thus the salads and water, rather than something richer. Yoga twice a day. Weights several times a week. Swimming daily.

She was in better shape than both of her sons, and more likely to turn heads than either of her daughters.

If the hair was mostly gray underneath the regular dye these days, that was the cost of growing older. The crow's feet around the eyes or the spots on the hands were the same way.

She could mask them, and did, but they were there in the morning when she rose.

One of these days, she would need to pick an heir, marry off the other three, and maybe just retire to life as a sailor and hotelier. Not a great change from now, but it would remove those moments when Tömörbaatar walked up with his serious face and waited for her to speak.

Most of them, anyway.

Behnam nodded for him to speak.

"A visitor, Your Grace," he said in that quiet, knowing voice.

The man had been at her side for more than thirty years now. If he was a squishy, past-middle-aged bureaucrat with a wispy beard gone gray, Tömörbaatar was still deadly in the political arena.

He would not speak lightly.

"Representing?" she replied.

No single visitor was that important, except as a symbol of something larger.

"A *Concord* naval captain," her man said. "Alone, but for a small staff, and traveling on official business. He made proper reservations through the system to spend a week, and made it clear that he would like an hour or two in private with you on a topic he would not discuss with anyone else. Myself included."

Altai was well outside the *Concord*. Her ship was not in *Concord* space now. If that stellar nation had chosen, they might have turned themselves into an empire, but they were content to leave most planets alone.

Shangdu itself was heavily armed, and flew with escorts at all times, because piracy recognized no political bounds.

The *Concord* could ask, but not demand. All that they could do by trying was to cause enmity with their much-smaller neighbors.

Behnam wondered if their spies had learned about Navarre's plans. *Hammerfield* could be traced to her, eventually, if you wanted to wade through legal structures designed to delight librarians with their obscurity. Navarre as well, especially since they had taken the vessel into *Concord* space as part of the man's revenge.

Still, this stranger had come alone, instead of bringing a warship. And asked politely.

And she might need their forbearance in the near future, once Navarre got truly ugly.

"Set up a working dinner for tomorrow night," she decided crisply. "Match his staff for size with yours. Assume brandy for either two or four afterwards."

"As Your Dread Grace commands," Tömörbaatar said with a grin, rising and nodding.

Behnam grinned back.

She had known the man for more than forty years. Watched him uphold her throne for thirty-one of them.

One *Concord* captain would not intimidate the *Iron Hero*.

And if it became necessary, she could always have the stranger killed.

That was the quiet power that came with being the *Khatum*.

SHE STUDIED the man as he sat across from her in the small dining hall she had arranged for this private dinner. He had worn a nice, green uniform that showed Zakhar Sokolov's origins.

Behnam could have seated two hundred in the Grand Hall, or chosen the room where four were crowded. Tonight, she had chosen a dining space as might serve most bankers' private residences, six meters long by nine wide, and dominated by an antique, oak table, at least nine centuries old.

It was the sort of room where ten could sit comfortably. Wood paneling waist-high around the room, with wallpaper above that to a semi-vaulted ceiling five meters up. Forest patterns and ocean scenes were worked into the patterns. Cedar beams running overhead, as if holding the arched ceiling up, when they were in fact deep in the safest part of the ship.

Hardwood floors almost cherry colored, sealed and shining, with a large, red rug under the table.

Homey.

Just the place for her to work out the stranger's intentions.

Captain Ayokunle was only a few years older than her, but looked every bit of a man in his sixth decade, where Behnam knew she could pass for thirty. Her beauty was just another weapon she might use to disarm and distract the man. Any man.

He had been a most charming dinner companion. Behnam was used to men and women who were filled with their own wealth and glory and rarely educated beyond the basics of business and enough economics to not lose their heritage.

This captain was trained as a historian, and had a lovely speaking voice. She wondered if all *Concord* officers were so charming. Navarre and Sokolov certainly were. She could add this man to the list.

Semi-invisible staff finished clearing the remains of dessert from the table. Tonight, she had chosen a simple meal, vegetable plates of escalating complexity of flavor mixed with occasional meat dishes to cleanse the palette. Topped with a blueberry ice cream she had asked the kitchen to make special for tonight.

Conversation had been polite and vague. Gossip, mostly, until she discovered the man's interest in history, and then Behnam had asked for stories.

It was a test. They all were, but Captain Ayokunle had risen to the challenge with relish.

But all good things come to an end.

"I think it is time, Captain," Behnam began, reaching out to grab a freshly-poured glass of Malbec. She nodded to the woman at Ayokunle's right, obviously an important aide, whereas the other two were mostly junior flunkies along to handle paperwork and errands. "The four of us should retire to a salon and get to business."

Ayokunle nodded serenely, holding his own glass and delicately sliding his chair back to rise.

It was a mark of professionalism, how quickly the room emptied of all but her, Ayokunle, Tömörbaatar, and the quiet woman in the uniform of a *Concord* Lt. Commander who only spoke in reply to direct questions, and had otherwise watched the rest of the meal pass in silence.

A professional spy who was still on duty, obviously.

The *Khatum* led them through a door into the salon that had been placed here for expressly the purpose of allowing the principals to retire after a meal for serious talk. Or bedtime stories, when her children had been much younger.

Three couches lined the walls, ranging from a thin, futon model with a blue cotton cover; to a grander, more traditional one that would hold four comfortably; to the overstuffed, red leather piece on the far wall that was excellent for making pillow forts, or conducting quiet affairs.

Behnam seated herself on the futon and went into a full lotus. It centered her mind and subtly distracted people with her flexibility, especially as she had chosen tight, green leggings tonight, soft moccasins, and a loose tunic in gray silk that clung in just the right places and gapped occasionally in distracting ways.

How better to deal with a stuffy *Concord* captain, even if he had turned out to be more like Navarre and Sokolov than the ones she was used to?

"Thank you," Ayokunle said as he took a spot on the middle couch, to her left, carefully holding his wine glass aloft as he settled himself.

"For?" she asked, matching his smile.

"Other places would treat this as a formal, diplomatic function," he replied. "Stale and dry. Much dancing about and evasion on the hopes we would become distracted or disgusted and depart in a huff."

"Oh?" she teased in a light tone. "Was that an option?"

"Probably not," he laughed in response. "But I wanted to show my appreciation for the option to handle this task quickly and quietly."

Behnam nodded in recognition. Captain Ayokunle was correct, on a variety of angles.

"I spoke with Captain Sokolov at *Merankorr*," the man said simply.

Behnam wasn't surprised by the revelation. And after an hour of listening to this man regale her with interesting tidbits, she was also not surprised that he would drop into his business quickly.

The whole point of dinner was to get all the small talk out of the way. Captain Ayokunle had apparently recognized that.

Still, she watched him like a hawk anyway, knowing that Tömörbaatar was tracking the aide, the spy, just as closely.

She waited with a vague smile for him to continue.

"Captain Sokolov is a bit of a mystery," the captain continued. "But one I was able to perhaps solve, at least a little."

"How so?" she asked.

If he had solved some mystery around Sokolov, knowing would help her. If nothing else, perhaps better blackmail on the man, although she doubted that. Certainly, more insight into his mysterious masters: the Jarre Foundation.

Ayokunle eyed her carefully, as if measuring his words against her intent.

"It was a surprise for me," Ayokunle said. "At *Merankorr*, that is. I knew the man much earlier, when we were both cadets at the *Bryce Academy* forty years ago. He had a different name then."

"I can't imagine that any pirate goes by his real name," she replied, just a touch breathless.

It wouldn't do to dissuade the man from keeping his secrets.

"Just so," Ayokunle said. "However, putting pieces together, I purchased the remnants of the ship that Sokolov was delivering for recasting. Sokolov wouldn't confirm it, but the vessel was *Storm Gauntlet*, his own previous vessel."

"And, Captain Ayokunle?" Behnam probed.

"And now he is in command of a First-Rate-Galleon," the man replied. "Of a type *Neu Berne* used to manufacture a century ago. And Sokolov claims you are a part owner of the vessel."

Behnam smiled. Perhaps the *Concord* had fallen for the cover story and dug no deeper, save what this man could find out. It would be a delicious outcome to a twisted story.

She might even tell him the truth, one of these years.

Not today.

"An investor," she said in a tired voice. "Nothing more. Navarre owns the warship. Sokolov provided the crew. I supplied some minimal amount of funding to help bridge expenses, for an under-capitalized venture with promise. Too many of those fail for not grasping the time frames necessary to achieve profitability."

Ayokunle's eyes slitted suddenly, like a cat sniffing the air.

"I see," the man obviously did not. "And their current intentions?"

"Eventually?" she replied. "Exploration. Establishing new trade routes and trading partners to benefit *Altai*. Profit."

"Eventually," he observed in a dry tone. "And in the meantime? It is our understanding that *Storm Gauntlet* as a vessel frequently engaged in activities that would be considered piracy in a *Concord* court."

Behnam focused a shark's smile on the man like a spotlight.

"Navarre did mention settling an old score."

She let that dangle in the air, a worm on a sharp hook. Interestingly, the spy woman stirred, after remaining so still that she might have been dozing.

"Commander?" Behnam purred, bringing the woman into the conversation.

Altai maintained an espionage service. It came with all manner of branches, from quiet killers like Farouz Jashari, currently accompanying Navarre, to public relations experts capable of bringing down entire hostile governments without a single shot being fired.

The other woman picked her words with the care of a diamond cutter.

"Intelligence reports suggest a crisis between two major criminal organizations," she said diplomatically.

"You are referring to Walvisbaai and Jarre?" Behnam inquired, placing herself on the same chess board as the *Concord* officers.

The spy nodded carefully.

"And you wish to know my part?" Behnam continued. "Why I have chosen sides?"

Both of them nodded in reply.

No, I will not tell you the truth. But I will share enough that you will perhaps be satisfied. For now.

She took a sip of wine and then set the glass down on a side table.

"Someone hired Navarre to steal something from one of my guests," she began in a serious tone. "Presumably, they were expecting a bloodbath, based on the man's reputation for extreme violence. What Navarre referred to as a *Mass Casualty Incident.* When he was successful without anyone being killed, that same person hired Walvisbaai to kill Navarre and Sokolov."

"Valko Slavkov," the woman spy said precisely. "*Svalbard.*"

"Yes," Behnam replied. "Your intelligence is good. Captain Navarre is possessed of a great rage. When his revenge is complete, both men intend to retire from their current occupations and become peaceful merchants."

"His revenge?" Ayokunle asked in a voice suddenly shakier than it had been.

Even the spy had shivered at her words.

Behnam smiled.

"And you know what he has planned?" the captain continued.

"Only that Navarre plans to live up to his reputation with this one," she said with an ugly chill in her voice. "Make an example of people. As he had told me, he only kills pirates."

"Is there any way to stop them?" the spy asked.

Behnam turned back to the captain.

"You said you knew Sokolov?" she asked. "How well?"

"He almost ended up as my brother-in-law," the man said

quietly. "Was the best man at my wedding, but I hadn't seen him in seventeen years, prior to this. I have questions for him, both personally and professionally. He and Navarre are in a dangerous spot. They might need friends."

She watched the man's face turn inward. Judged him based on all the bits and pieces he had revealed over the course of a lovely evening.

Made a decision.

"They will be returning here very briefly," she said. "I will hold you out of touch with your superiors until they depart, but I will allow you to meet them. Perhaps something fruitful will come of it."

The look of hope on the man's face told her that she had made the right decision, just as much as the sourness from the spy woman did.

She would see Navarre and Sokolov shortly.

Hopefully, it wouldn't be for the last time.

PART TWO

Javier entered *Hammerfield's* bridge through the monstrous, reinforced portal designed by some naval architect with delusions of adequacy.

Seriously. It should have been the same plain gray-green as everything else on this ship, and standard height and width. This stupid thing was an extra fifty centimeters wider, a whole meter taller, and banded with extra straps of a golden metal running vertically in three places.

Said moron had decided that the bridge access should remind everyone of a bank vault. And some other moron had agreed with the first one.

One of these days, he would rip the damned thing out and replace it with a standard model.

Actually, come to think of it, what he should do is knock out some interior crawlspaces, gut this enormous cathedral of space, and replace it with an arena of some sort, with a space for athletic events in the center, and maybe a stage, or a stage in the round, where musicians or theater companies could perform. At twenty-seven meters across the circle, and nine meters tall at the peak, it would be doable.

After all, Suvi was flying the ship. And she didn't need anyone else's help, but preferred to have a couple of folks handy, mostly for chatting. They could move everyone down to command and support things from the Auxiliary Bridge on deck eight and probably nobody would notice.

But one look at Zakhar, shaved head gleaming, seated atop his command throne like Zeus, reminded Javier of how unlikely it was that the man would give up that feeling of utter godhead that came with the design of *Hammerfield*'s bridge. Plus, a smaller space would limit the options for a big crew reunion.

The whole gang was here: Zakhar as Zeus, which probably made Piet Mercury, or something. Mary-Elizabeth would be Mars, or maybe Athena, depending on how the gunner was feeling today.

No, strike that. Definitely Athena. Mars was seated at Zakhar's right hand, knitting. Like a spider weaving her web. Which wasn't fair, since Djamila had really dialed the crazed militancy down a number of notches over the last few months. But once an image got into Javier's head…

Andreea Dalca would be down in engineering as Hephaestus, brooding over her gigantic eggs with Afia close by.

Javier waved at Piet and Zakhar as he moved to his station and powered everything up. A science officer didn't have much of anything to do in jump since the ship existed in its own pocket dimension and the scanners were worthless.

Scientists had postulated that all ships entering hyperspace actually traveled in the same dimension, but since they were moving FTL relative to everything, including each other, nobody had ever figured out a way to see each other, let alone chat.

Javier sat, hooked his seatbelt, and blew a silent kiss at Suvi's image, top among all the faces down the left side of his screen. She blushed and curtsied. And then, because she was a complete and utter goof, stuck her tongue out at him.

It was a good thing she could display a different image on all the other screens.

"Seven minutes to emergence," Piet announced, mostly just to have something to say.

In hyperspace, he had about as much to do as the science officer.

"Javier," Zakhar said across the space, drawing Javier's head around to look up at the captain.

"Are we completely insane for doing this?"

Javier shrugged. Wasn't the first time this conversation had gone back and forth. Just less yelling and gesticulating this time. Public company and all that.

"Son of a bitch has never been told no," Javier said. "Never been put in a situation where someone could push back. Never had *consequences* become uncomfortable."

"I get Slavkov," Zakhar replied. "What about Walvisbaai?"

"I'm sorry," Javier said in a heavy, ugly growl. "Did you just suggest that one of the worst pirate organizations in the galaxy *doesn't* have it coming?"

"There might be innocents," Zakhar countered.

"No," Javier commented with a hard snap. "These are people who have enjoyed a comfortable living making others victims. Taking slaves and selling them to mining colonies or other terminal destinations. Destroying peoples' dreams and their livelihoods. Making the galaxy a nastier place."

"And you're going to fix all that, on your own?" Zakhar asked.

"I took an oath as a *Concord* officer," Javier said simply.

There wasn't much more to it than that. The good guys. Protectors of the innocent and helpless. Paladins on charging steeds. Protectors of the galaxy.

If they had failed, it wasn't for lack of commitment. Even from an ex-drunk, twice-divorced, former officer who had blown up his career before he'd finally managed to scrape together enough money to buy a retired probe-cutter and go explore the galaxy.

Before he had lost almost everything to pirates.

Javier could see the dark fire in the other man's eyes. Probably matched his own. They had both taken that oath a very long time ago.

"And afterwards?" Zakhar asked.

From the dead silence around them, Javier knew that the rest of the bridge crew was listening in. Hell, Suvi might be piping this to all compartments with folks awake.

What would come, the day after Armageddon.

"Afterwards, you folks get to decide whether or not to join me on a grand adventure," Javier said. "If we survive, we'll have political cover, firepower, reward money, and a significant chunk of the galaxy in front of us to explore. We just have to kill a lot of people first."

He and Zakhar locked eyes across the space.

It really did all come down to this.

It had always been there, even from that first moment they met, years ago, when Javier woke up in the man's office with his hands bound behind him and Sykora whomping him on the skull every time he got out of line.

He and Zakhar were the only two here who had been officers in the *Concord* Navy, since Suvi hadn't been there in that room, and even she had only been a yeoman.

Unspoken communication between two men of honor. Brothers-in-arms, wherever they met.

The Bryce Connection.

Was Zakhar willing to pay the price necessary to make the galaxy a better place, even if he had to kill a great number of people to do it?

Zakhar considered things, and then nodded. Just like that.

So little, and so much. They would take that to the end of civilized space and beyond. Around them, Javier heard crew members remember to breathe.

"Bridge, bring the ship to Red Alert," Zakhar ordered in that grand, captain's voice he did so well. "All hands to action stations."

"Confirming Red Alert, Captain," Suvi said in her quiet, professional voice.

"Affirmative," the man called. "We're about to drop out of space to meet the *Khatum*. Javier might trust her, but I don't. Unlock all weapon stations and prepare for combat. If nothing else, a good exercise to keep the crew awake."

Javier shook his head. Not exactly disbelief, but close enough for government work.

He was pretty sure he'd never figure out what made a man like Zakhar Sokolov tick.

Hell, he only barely understood his own foibles.

Around them, the lighting added a red tint and the stupid siren ah-OOO-ga'ed several times to wake the dead.

Well, maybe not the dead, considering all the century-old corpses of *Hammerfield's* former crew, carefully stowed away below. But everybody else would be moving like their ass was on fire.

And if it did turn out to be a double-cross from the *Khatum*, boy, wouldn't she be in for a surprise?

PART THREE

Power.

That's what this was.

Pure and unbridled power, something Zakhar hadn't had at his fingertips in a long time.

Storm Gauntlet had been a strike corvette. Hell on wheels against a freighter. Pretty good against torpedo boats and system patrol craft. Got her ass handed to her by *Ajax*, a *Raider-class* boat comparable to a heavy frigate or a destroyer.

Hammerfield was a First-Rate-Galleon. She could go toe to toe with most fleet's cruisers, and maybe take on a *Concord* Warmaster, depending on the class and age of the other guy.

Zakhar looked out from his elevated perch at the big display screen on the wall in front of him. Below him, arranged in a circle at their stations, the group he thought of as the *Inner Circle* of Centurions: Djamila, Mary-Elizabeth, Piet, Javier. Kibwe Bousaid, his communications expert and paperwork specialist with the smooth, radio voice who was close enough to count.

Even Suvi was fitting in with this group. But he ran a tight ship, along *Concord* lines, something she had been born and raised to.

"Thirty seconds to emergence," Piet said in a loud voice. "All stations ready for combat."

Piet was coming along as a First Officer. Javier probably would have done better, but that man was determined to go down a different path, as were they all.

The screens went live as *Hammerfield* returned to the real universe. Zakhar had wondered if ships that disappeared had just never come back out of hyperspace, even though he knew it was more likely that they had been captured by pirates.

Like him. Or, like he had been.

Before.

Zakhar had become a pirate from the necessity to pay the bills, unlike many of them. Abraam Tamaz had been *Storm Gauntlet*'s first officer, once, before that man turned truly evil. And gotten himself killed by Javier.

Good riddance.

Most pirates were like Tamaz that way. Folks that wanted to hurt other people for no particular reason. Bad, broken people.

Zakhar's command boards quickly filled with information. They had been to *Binhai* previously, so some things could be tracked and identified very quickly. Others would take longer, but there was only one ship he was really looking for.

Shangdu. The Pleasure Dome.

There.

Still in a very high orbit, hopefully innocently awaiting them, along with a handful of small escort craft to deal with whatever trouble might wander along. *Binhai* maintained her own system defenses, so anyone attacking would be facing death by a thousand paper cuts.

Still, nothing immediately challenged them or made to get close. Only a fool fought in low orbit, inside the gravity well.

Well, fools and the desperate. *Storm Gauntlet* had gotten away, but it had been close. And not everyone had survived the encounter, although the casualties could have been much worse.

"Comm, hail the system coordinator for an orbital lane assignment," Zakhar called to Kibwe. He knew Suvi would do the actual work, but his assistant would put the right flavor on the words. "Then call *Shangdu* and request a docking window for the shuttle."

"Aye, sir," Bousaid said in that warm baritone of his.

The faster they could drop off all the prisoners, the sooner he could move on with Javier's mad plan. And the sooner he could start thinking about *happily ever after.*

Zakhar was *The Captain.* He could have never approached Djamila, as much as they both wanted him to. And he hadn't believed that she would ever work up the courage to do it herself. But she had, with the help of Suvi and Afia, wonder of wonders.

If they all went fully legitimate, as they were planning on doing when this thing was done, then it was Javier's ship. Suvi's really. And he was just crew. Nothing unethical about that.

How long had it been since he had just been crew?

Back when he had been the pilot on the Concord *destroyer* Horizon. *Wow, that long?*

Zakhar shook his head and focused on the task at hand: a quick rendezvous with *Shangdu*, and then a date with eternity.

"Acknowledgement from *Shangdu*, sir," Kibwe said in a tone that brought Zakhar's head around. "Along with a private message for you from the *Khatum.*"

Me? Private message? What the hell?

Zakhar keyed the privacy field around his station and opened the message.

Damn, that woman just kept getting more beautiful every day.

Zakhar wondered briefly if she was a vampire or something.

"Captain Sokolov," she began with a warm smile that left him even colder. "A messenger came seeking you while you were gone. After interviewing him, and knowing that you would be returning after a short period, I asked him to remain, isolated from communicating with the outside world. I will make him available when you and Navarre arrive. I think you will look forward to the conversation."

There was another file attached to this one. A picture. Nguyên Ayokunle. Looking just as professional and competent as ever. And apparently a messenger.

Spy, more likely. But that was okay. They were well outside *Concord* space now and would remain so for a very long time.

And what was coming next was something the *Concord* would be interested in, no doubt.

Zakhar routed the message to Javier with a cover note.

This man was almost my brother-in-law.

Let him make of that what he would.

PART FOUR

SHANGDU.

Xanadu.

Zakhar had finally gotten around to reading the ancient poem about Kublai Khan's Pleasure Dome. The *Khatum of Altai* had certainly done an impressive job taking the concept and turning it into a starship.

Zakhar sat across a small table from Nguyên Ayokunle, both men dressed formally for the affair in uniforms that nearly mirrored one another, with Javier, Djamila, the *Khatum* herself, and her Prime Minister at her side. Or whatever the man was called.

He wasn't an assassin. Zakhar had met some of this woman's assassins. Hired them, even.

This one was a bureaucrat. Didn't make him one gram less dangerous.

Their table was on a semi-private balcony, overlooking the monstrous swimming pool she called a lake. An ellipse two kilometers long and one wide, with an artificial island in the center.

On a starship.

There was a breeze, coming out of what Zakhar would call

the northeast, given that the artificial sun overhead was just in the process of "setting" now.

Bizarre, but close enough to being on a planet, without all the bugs and crap. Probably better, at that, since she could control everything, and she could take it with her.

Rich people were weird.

But dinner had been amazing. Dessert as well. Nobody had drunk much, staying mostly with lemonade or water. Too much risk of alcohol causing more trouble than it was worth.

Yên hadn't changed in the last six weeks. Or probably the last twenty years, when you got right down to it. You could tell he still wanted to use a different name in conversation, but kept himself practicing with Zakhar.

He would probably slip at some point.

Zakhar shrugged in his head. He could keep being several people. Up until now, probably none of the other players had realized the truth, even as Javier played at being Navarre and Djamila occasionally appeared in public as Hadiiye.

Yên fixed him with that hard stare that made cadets wet themselves.

"She won't tell me anything," he said firmly, nodding at the *Khatum*.

"That's because we're not on the same side, Yên," Zakhar said in an even tone.

"I represent *The Concord*," he huffed.

"And we're pirates," Javier stepped into the conversation. "Start from there and work up."

Yên scowled at the interruption.

"The Jarre Foundation is not registered as a *Concord* organization," Zakhar interjected before the other two men got going. "Nor is Walvisbaai Industrial. The *Khatum of Altai* and Slavkov are also outside your jurisdiction, Yên."

"So I'm just supposed to sit here while you politely pat me on the head?" Yên rasped.

Zakhar would have liked to pick an alternative option, but there wasn't one. Just a man with a badge, and several other men and women with guns. Still, it was good to see his old friend, however stilted and awkward the conversation had to be.

"Yên, we're going to do something so brazen that nobody would believe us," Zakhar placated. "We'd rather you folks not upset the equation."

"What, Captain Sokolov?" the man asked with a sneer. "What could you be planning that OpSec silence is so critical?"

"We're going to break Walvisbaai," Javier said in a quiet tone. "Utterly destroy them. Salt the earth afterwards. You don't get to mess that up."

Zakhar shivered inwardly at the words. Yên blanched.

"You think I would interfere?" Yên asked.

"You aren't likely to help," Javier countered in a sharp tone. "So the best you might do is muddle things. You can clean up the pieces after we're long gone, Captain Ayokunle."

Zakhar was still getting used to the quiet, angry Javier Aritza. Captain Navarre was a cold-blooded, ruthless killer, but Javier had always been more of a goofball. A bright spot on the deck.

Zakhar suspected he was seeing the *Concord* officer as this man had once been. God help the universe if it made this version of the science officer angry.

Angrier.

Walvisbaai Industrial was already going to find out the hard way.

Yên turned his attention back to Zakhar.

"And you won't tell me anything?" he asked.

"Not today," Zakhar responded. "When it's all done and over, we might be on the same side again. Then we can talk."

"Might?"

"Yên," Zakhar finally let his exasperation show. "Zakhar Sokolov is a wanted criminal with a price on his head. You can't change that."

"Yes," the man agreed. "*Zakhar Sokolov* is. There are other options on the table."

"Pal, you haven't got the jets to swing that one," Javier sneered.

"Then who will protect you?" Yên asked.

Javier nodded to the *Khatum*.

"She will," he said.

"The *Khatum*?" Yên queried.

"In addition to being an early investor, there were other considerations," the woman said in that voice that flowed like warm honey.

"Such as?"

"Letters of Marque and Reprisal," her tone was no less taut than Javier's. No less angry.

Yên twitched at the implications.

"Yes," she continued, voice turning cold and sharp. "Valko Slavkov decided to make me an enemy. Walvisbaai chose to help him. Captain Navarre is going to break both of them for me."

Even Zakhar shivered a little at the viciousness in her voice.

She and Navarre/Aritza seemed well-matched. Zakhar wondered if the galaxy would survive.

Yên slowly turned his head to study each face around him, including the two silent ones. Finally, he spoke.

"Then will you at least tell me where to go, to help pick up the pieces?"

"No," Javier was blunt. "Watch the evening news when the reporters finally release the footage. We'll be long gone by then."

Zakhar watched the energy flow angrily between the two men. Time to step in, before it got out of hand.

"Yên," Zakhar said. "I know you mean well. And I know where to find you, or at least get a message. One of these days, we'll talk. I promise."

That placated him. Some.

Everyone lapsed into silence as the sun finally "set" and automatic lights came up to brighten the artificial twilight.

Zakhar hoped it wasn't a metaphor for what was coming.

Behnam sat carefully on her end of the oversized couch and watched the man. This had been his suite, both times he had stayed here on her ship.

She had begun to think of it as his.

The spare bedrooms for bodyguards the man no longer kept, if he ever had. The pale, blue, main bedroom for snuggling. The marble bathtub comfortable for two. The multi-level green and brown salon, with the bar to one side, where all manner of assignations and meetings could be held.

Creator knew that the man wasn't likely to come to her chambers. Even for one night.

Captain Navarre was never going to be happy just living at *Shangdu*. Too quiet a life, and at the same time, too many people.

It was an odd combination in anyone, and one she barely understood, but Behnam was beginning to know the man under the terrible façade of the killer pirate.

She kept her feet curled under her and a glass of spiced port in one hand. He was close enough to touch, with his shoes tossed casually away as he had entered, and his legs up on the sofa, pointed at her.

Navarre had a glass of the port as well, but was actually

drinking his, where she just sipped at hers for show.

Finally, his eyes focused on her. Something locked in, like an ambush predator perched on a branch as prey went by below.

It brought an exciting shiver to Behnam's soul, him watching her like that. She had no other way to describe it.

Not lust. Or rather, not just lust. Respect. Regret. Possibly even softer emotions, if a man that could present Eutrupio Navarre to the outer world was capable of soft sentiments.

He had a hard face. Masculine and square. Just graying around the edges in a way that suggested a man in his early forties. So perhaps half a decade younger that her, but possessed of far more light years than she had.

One eyebrow went up, framing his inquisitive brown eyes, but he remained silent.

He would not start the conversation, this quiet, dangerous man. But she knew that already. Navarre was a man of sudden action and perfect stillness. Much like Farouz Jashari. Both men killers in their own right.

"Do you have a death wish?" Behnam asked simply.

She tried to convey the question warmly, but it was a cold way to start any conversation.

Navarre studied her closely before answering.

The moment stretched, but she would not break the spider web. That communication rang silently between them. And he knew that.

Had she ever met a man capable of using silence as a weapon so effectively?

"Navarre does not," he replied finally, slowly.

"And the other man?" she asked. "The one you are when you are not Navarre? What is he like? Has he a deathwish?"

Again, silence. Weighing his words with care.

"He did, I think," the man said, barely above a whisper.

"Did?"

"Did," Navarre agreed. "Blew up two marriages with his drinking and stupidity. And a career as a *Concord* officer. Was circling the drain. Slowly, but surely. Then I met Suvi."

"And would you consider her your third wife?" Behnam

asked carefully, fully aware that she had moved onto new ground with this man. Possibly safe. Possibly ice.

She had spoken with Suvi when this mission started. Gotten some of that woman's side of things, and some of what had transpired. Without ever naming names.

"My only daughter," he said with a sudden smile. "I had to be responsible, for once. Get over myself. Grow up, I suppose."

He took a long, contemplative drink of his port.

"Discover a reason to go on living that was more than just the next round of drinks," he concluded.

Behnam leaned forward. Just a touch.

She had worn a low-cut blouse to dinner. Navy blue silk, crossing two pieces from shoulder to opposite hip and wrapping around her.

It belled out. Not much.

Enough that she could watch his eyes flicker down and then back up.

"And now?" she asked, letting her voice add a hint of breathlessness she knew he would appreciate. "Do you have reasons to survive?"

He grinned, ever so slightly.

"Perhaps," he whispered.

"Perhaps?" she asked, leaning a little farther, letting the gap in her top swell out a little more.

Again, his eyes flickered. Lingered longer. Climbed hesitantly back up to her face.

"There will be vendettas after this," he observed. "Many people will be extremely angry. The powerful will be the most helpless. The powerless may have nothing to lose."

Behnam unfurled her legs, turning them sideways so that she could drape herself across the back of the green sofa. A masterpiece by one of the Greeks, perhaps.

"So you will need shelter," she replied. "Someplace to come in from the rain and darkness."

"It will be cold in the depths of space," Navarre said.

"And you will have no one to warm you?" she asked. "Just your *Sentience* for company?"

Now the ice would grow thin under her feet.

Behnam had discussed the topic with Suvi, who seemed to know far more than anyone gave her credit for. Being the very ship around them made that easy.

Navarre had many mistresses among the crew. Only Hadiiye and a few others had never spent a night in his bed. But Suvi didn't think any of them had ever altered his behavior.

Ever touched his soul.

Navarre was a man like an iceberg. Moving with casual deliberation. Mostly submerged and invisible. Utterly implacable once he was set on a path.

Behnam supposed many would be driven under the waves, ground under an implacable wall of ice, attempting to resist.

But then, she had not taken up monasticism, either, so she could not demand it of him.

Not yet, anyway.

She could tell from his words that he expected this mission to be his death.

Going down fighting, in a battle he had chosen to wage.

Paladin.

"Space can be very lonely," he said finally, after letting the silence build like a static charge.

She was closer to him now. Not touching, but able to feel his warmth.

Navarre carefully set his glass on the floor, and then took hers as well.

She placed one hand on his chest.

Navarre might look calm, but she could count the rapid beats of his heart.

She let the silence build like a spiderweb.

Behnam leaned forward to kiss Navarre once. Light.

One hand came up and encircled her shoulders, his hands warm.

She snuggled into the crook of his arm and let the man's fire give lie to his words.

She would have this one night with the man.

Tomorrow, she had to send him off to die.

BOOK TWENTY-SIX: DEEP SPACE

Javier knew the look that the woman had in her eyes. Knew it all too well.

Afia was going to be a pain on this one. Stubborn. Unflinching. My-way-or-the-highway kind of argument over precedent and personality.

He took a deep breath and closed his eyes. Today was not the day for this.

She knew that. He knew that.

Hell, everyone knew that.

At least they weren't on a deadline. Then he might have just thrown the tiny woman over his shoulder and carried her off like a kidnapping in broad daylight. He could have lived with the kicking and screaming. And the biting and cussing.

Afia apparently knew that.

She just smiled serenely up at him.

"Because I'm right," she beamed at him. "And you damned well know it, Javier."

And he did. Which just made it worse.

"I appreciate your sense of ownership on the topic," he replied, trying to budge her one centimeter. "And the two weeks here in the middle of bloody nowhere when the rest of us got to go off and play at *Shangdu*. And thank you for seeing it done right. But this is my mission."

"What's the phrase you mutter under your breath?" she asked innocently. "Oh, yes. *Screw you, princess. This one's mine.*"

Javier was taken slightly aback. Not far. Afia Burakgazi wouldn't have been here, now, if she wasn't smart, capable, and stubborn as a Missouri mule. Or a Yukon grizzly.

Pixie grizzly?

He fought not to grin at the image.

Serious business. Pain-in-the-ass engineer. The worst kind.

One who was right.

This was either going to be over quickly, or they would be at it all day. Better to find out now, when he could still figure out how much beer he needed.

"Why?" he asked bluntly.

"You want that list alphabetical, chronological, or by degree of difficulty?" she smirked up at him.

Seriously, a woman a head shorter than him shouldn't be smirking like that. Plus, that question was usually asked naked and sweaty. Which was the best way to enjoy it.

Afia was going to be a pain, obviously.

"By color," he replied, willing to dance with the tiny dynamo today.

It wasn't like anything was going to happen until this got sorted out.

He took a moment to find the captain's chair and settle himself in, looking once around the big bridge for strength.

They had re-christened the Land Leviathan's transport as *Odysseus*. It was a rude inside joke about how the Hellenes won the Trojan War.

With a trick horse.

Javier didn't put much truck in the original story, but it made for a fanciful image.

Afia walked over after him, kipped her leg up, and rested a hip on the console.

Javier found it amusing that both of them checked to see that the boards were cold before her butt made contact.

Engineers to the core.

The big picture window behind her was unshielded, showing a field of black space speckled with occasional stars in the far distance. Javier and Zakhar had purposefully parked the stolen ship in the darkness between two systems, so nobody accidentally found them.

Afia and her small crew of engineering lunatics had spent their time fixing the ship up for her final mission.

The storming of Ilium.

She looked down at him like she saw Achilles.

Hopefully not. Javier was too beautiful to die so young, even if he would leave a fantastic corpse and one hell of a story.

"I'm just guessing here," she began, lowering her tone.

They were alone on the bridge, with all the rest of everyone either over on *Hammerfield* getting ready, or down in the big transport bay aft, working on things, or back in engineering.

Just the two of them. To argue it out.

Javier fixed her with a good dose of stinkeye. She was as immune as all the other people he had tried it on recently. Must be losing his touch.

"This was one of the things that you didn't like about being an officer, back in your navy days," she continued.

Javier pelted the woman with silence. Easiest way to keep her talking was to not interrupt.

"Sending someone else off to maybe die, or screw up monumentally," she said. "When you knew you could do the job at least as well, if not better."

Javier felt his scowl turn sour. Thunderous.

Hard.

"You don't trust that I'm good enough to do this," she said in a flat, accusatory tone.

He started to move. To heave himself up out of the amazingly comfortable chair the previous captain had installed and get right into her face.

Afia forestalled him by reaching out one hand and pushing him back down into the chair, at the same time interrupting his words.

"Or you don't want to live with the guilt of sending someone you like off to die," she snapped.

Javier subsided.

Damned, stubborn engineers.

Especially when she was right.

Javier had always been one of the best engineering officers he knew, even when he was on a command track.

Way too much of an extrovert to fit down with the big machines and quiet people.

But she was right.

Guilt at sending kids into a failing reactor, and challenging them to die in single combat with a runaway system spewing out a lethal mixture of radiation, heat, and shrapnel.

Knowing they were never coming out of that room alive.

And that the best they could do would be to insure that nobody else had to go in after them and die, pushing the rock another meter up the hill, until either Javier ran out of men, or the ship exploded.

The second batch of kids had eventually succeeded in slaying the beast.

The drinking had started that night. As did the nightmares.

More than a decade would pass before he escaped either of them.

He really didn't want to go back there.

Especially not with Afia.

"It's okay," she whispered, reaching out a hand to catch the tears suddenly streaming down his face.

Javier just sat perfectly still and tried to hold onto his horizons as they threatened to turn upside down again.

He finally remembered to breathe.

"I can't order you off this ship when we get there, can I?" he finally asked in a defeated, wan voice.

"Nope," she chirped. "And Djamila would tackle you instead of me, if push came to shove. You know that, right?"

"Yeah," he let go a sigh.

She was right.

"Good," Afia Burakgazi, Combat Engineer, pronounced. "Then we're going to do this my way."

Javier sucked cool air all the way down into his big toes.

Damn this woman. Damn all engineers.

"Walk me through it," Javier said, trying to find solace in their shared nerdiness. "From the top."

She smiled. It was warm, and sad, and knowing. He wondered if Suvi had told Afia too much. Not that his sidekick knew everything, but someone else might have mentioned something at some point. Or he might have screamed in a nightmare and forgotten it by morning.

The dark places in his head were unfit for even him. Let alone innocent strangers.

"We'll come out of the terminal jump with a soft head of steam," Afia began. "One last course correction to line up the cue ball, and then the assault team bails. Scuttling charges are set to five minutes. Assault team hits the lifeboat and runs like hell. Everything is physics at that point."

"And the scuttle?" he asked.

"In case someone over there reacts fast enough to think they can stop us," she smiled grimly. "You, me, and Suvi are an evil combination, but Djamila is just flat rude when she puts her mind to it."

"That's why I put up with her," he said quietly. "Life boat packed?"

"Affirmative," she acknowledged. "We'll be over an inhabitable planet, if worst comes to absolute worst. Guns, fake IDs, cover stories, and money already in place. Your job is to pull an avenging angel with the eclipse attack and pick our butts up before the bad guys get there."

"That's what I'm planning," Javier said.

"Well," Afia replied. "This ought to go down in history as the…what was the term you used?"

"*Le Beau Geste*," Javier said. "The Grand Gesture."

Yeah, nobody was ever forgetting this one.

And if he did it right, there wouldn't be that many survivors available to eventually come after him.

Turner didn't like it, but there wasn't much choice in the matter. Not after the way she had screwed up at *Svalbard*, letting Navarre and *Storm Gauntlet* get away.

Ajax nearly getting gutted in the encounter hadn't helped, even if Captain Sokolov had that kind of a reputation.

At least the repairs had gone well, as slow as the process had been to finally get her ship in and have it assayed. *Ajax* was as good as new.

Now, she just had to figure out why her boss had instructed her to call on him in person. Aboard the main station.

Walvisbaai Industrial Platform Number One.

Home port. The biggest non-*Concord* shipyard in the entire sector. The galaxy's principal chop shop.

A massive spindle, like a strange, child's top, flying slowly across the sky. And it was all business: manufacturing, service, and repair. The brothels and such were down on the planet, with a constant stream of shuttles running people up and down the gravity well or out to the other stations, where simple spacers lived.

Almost nobody lived on the Platform itself, except the important muckety-mucks at Walvisbaai. The *Made* Men and Women. And even then, few actually lived there. They just kept apartments and boltholes, safe from assassins that might hide in the general population of a planet.

Always traveling with bodyguards and gunboats.

Turner faced the door at the end of the hallway with a moment of trepidation, but it opened as she stopped moving.

She entered.

At least there was no plastic sheeting on the floor. That was always a concern when dealing with people that had offices like this: the penthouse suite at the very northern tip of the station.

"Captain Kowalski, come in," the man's voice rang out.

Turner was amazed at the size of the room. She could have parked a landing shuttle in here with room on all sides.

One wall was transparent, floor to three-meter ceiling, running a curve at least forty meters wide. Turner could just make out the distant, gleaming star that was *Ayakot Station*, *Ajax*'s actual home when they were here, warriors not being welcome on the industrial grounds that made Walvisbaai's money.

Thick shag carpet in cream covered the floor. Sand-colored paint made all the walls look more distant, somehow. Like she was on the surface of a planet in the middle of a desert, or something.

Real, honest wooden desk to one side. One meter tall, meter and a half deep, two meters wide. Maybe oak, considering. Two chairs on this side, neither of them looking comfortable. That would be the couch off to her left, closer to the wetbar. Presumably where guests would be entertained.

Turner wondered if her fate was the desk, or the bar. The man who had ordered her here had a reputation as the most lethal accountant in the galaxy.

Looking at him, it was hard to see. Dillon Toov was short, round, bald, and swarthy. Even the fantastically expensive suit only barely made him look like what he really was: one of Walvisbaai Industrial's Board of Directors.

The dangerous eleven men and women at the top of the pyramid.

Turner began to walk across the vast space to where Toov sat behind his desk. She fixed a polite smile on her face and tried not to think about gunmen stepping out from behind a pillar to shoot her in the back for whatever imagined failure had brought her here.

If it wasn't big, they could have sent her a message pack.

The personal touch probably meant it was bad.

"Sit," Toov ordered, gesturing to one of the rigid metal chairs with minimal padding.

Turner planted herself and tried to relax. Every sound behind her was a pistol cocking.

Dillon Toov didn't help her frame of mind by silently watching her, a predator's eye deep in a pool of still water.

Thirty seconds passed. Turner managed to not fidget.

Not too passive. Not too aggressive. Keep it professional and polite.

"There are those who think you have lost it," Toov began. "Are no longer good enough to maintain your place in the pack hierarchy."

Turner listened, trying not to clench her shoulder blades together before the beam struck.

"The damage to *Ajax* was extensive," he continued. "And expensive to repair. Your numbers this year will be atrocious, as a result."

She nodded. Two months in drydock, shimming in an early engine overhaul and weapons upgrade to the repairs *Ajax* had already suffered.

How well did they love her? Enough to overlook being outdueled by Sokolov?

"The Board discussed replacing you," Toov dangled that tidbit out there.

Turner nodded again. As the commander of *Ajax*, she was one of their top fighting officers. Her fate would be a topic of great interest.

How many of them would be on her side?

Toov just watched her.

Turner had been focused on the man's face. Still was, but noticed that the desk had papers stacked neatly in three piles.

Antique ink pens in a used coffee mug to one side. Screen built into the desktop, but turned off. Another mug by his left hand, faint wisps of steam coming off of it.

Toov reached out and grabbed his mug. Coffee, she suspected, from the smell.

He sipped, still watching her like a crocodile.

Toov put the mug back down with a small thump.

"Good," he said in a much more jovial tone. "No pleading. No arguing. No defensiveness."

He pushed his chair back and rose. Turner watched him move to the wetbar and gesture for her to join him.

"Come."

The bulk was misleading. As she got close, she remembered that Dillon Toov was her height, average for a man. The roundness only made him seem short. He carried an extra thirty kilograms of soft mass around like padding, but the man still moved like a shark.

She was taller than most of the women she knew. At forty-two, the lush curves were starting to get out of hand enough that she had to change her diet and workout routine so she could slim down and tone up. Some men liked a mature woman, but Turner knew she was past the age where big boobs and blond hair was enough to turn a man's head.

Fortunately, she had brains to back it all up. And the ruthlessness to become a captain in an organization that was heavily tilted towards men in charge.

Toov moved around behind the bar and pulled out a bottle and two glasses.

He filled both with something midway between amber and plum. It smelled sweet.

One glass went to her, and he took the other.

"The final vote was nine to two in favor of keeping you, Turner," he announced with a shark smile, sipping.

Turner took a sip as well. Something like sake, but with a fruity undertaste that went long and slow.

This one bottle was probably worth as much as she made in a month, knowing the scales Walvisbaai Industrial worked at.

Nine to two? Really?

The alcohol worked magic on her nerves and muscles. Turner felt a centimeter taller just letting everything inside relax.

"But now we have a different problem," Toov continued. "I want your opinion in a setting without anyone around to give you pause."

You mean, besides you?

She held herself perfectly still. Toov had only implied that he had been part of the nine, and not the two. She could only guess.

"Something interesting happened to Valko Slavkov while you were here," he explained.

Turner let her eyes and face speak. Powerful men frequently just liked to hear themselves talk. She had learned she could indulge them and often hear more than they intended.

"Somebody stole his car," Toov concluded.

"They what?" Turner shot out, surprise coloring her body language.

"Someone managed to hijack the freighter carrying his prize tank," Dillon Toov smirked. "*The Land Leviathan*. It took off on schedule from its most recent stop, headed this direction for a major overhaul. But it never appeared at the first jump point."

Turner blinked in shock as the size of such an operation unfolded in her mind. And the sheer brass. And the subtlety to pull it off and then vanish.

"How long ago?" she asked.

"Four weeks," Toov replied. "The two escorts, Slavkov's gunboats, ran a full search pattern, tracking as much as they could locate, before they came here, hoping that the freighter had managed to somehow make it anyway. No dice."

Turner nodded.

They were all pirates. It was a business, but it was also a profession. She could appreciate a professional job.

"Who has he pissed off the most?" she asked.

Toov took another drink and shrugged eloquently.

"Everybody?" he said. "Nobody? That's why I wanted to speak with you privately."

"Sir?" she said, careful with even the non-verbal communication.

"Looking at the records, Slavkov's most recent issues were with Navarre and Sokolov," Toov said. "And by extension, the Jarre Foundation."

"*Svalbard*," she replied, trying to keep her anger under tight rein.

Svalbard, where Navarre and a surprise, heavy combat team had taken out her entire ground force, and then had the audacity to capture them and return them unharmed. Where Zakhar Sokolov had managed to evade Turner's every gambit, out-duel her in the darkness, and then somehow teleport a torpedo into a position where she had to let him escape, just to give her own crew a chance to kill the incoming missile before it killed her.

And it had been a close thing.

Toov nodded.

"I've read your reports," he said. "Actually watched some of the footage of the battle and your crew debriefs. Sokolov's good. Navarre is a complete wildcard. And they have finally reappeared."

"Have they now?" Turner purred.

She owed those two men a serious ass-kicking for *Svalbard*. It would be nice to finally balance the books.

"Before you get your hopes up, Turner, there is a problem," Toov replied.

She bit back the tart response lurking on the tip of her tongue. He might still be part of the two, and not the nine.

"They've stolen a warship this time," he continued. "A big one."

"A warship?" she asked.

Navarre was developing a reputation as a magician. Sokolov was a meat-and-potatoes kind of guy, but extremely capable as a ship-handler. Dangerous, dangerous combination.

"Understand I am not a naval officer," Toov said.

Turner nodded.

"According to our spies, the vessel is called a First-Rate-Galleon," Toov concluded.

"Son of a bitch!" Turner exploded. "How dare he?"

"Bad?" Toov looked concerned.

"Huge, armed cargo vessel with the firepower of a cruiser," she snarled. "Nobody's made any new ones that I'm aware of in decades. Not since the end of the Great War. Way too big for *Ajax* to take on, maybe our entire fleet. You'll have to send assassins, next time."

"Personal affront, Turner?" Toov asked soothingly.

"I owe both of those men," she snarled. "No way for me to collect if they can swat *Ajax* like a fly."

"I see," Toov said, finishing off his glass and pouring two more fingers in. "But you agree that they might be behind this?"

"Navarre killed Tamaz and crew by himself," she recalled. "*Storm Gauntlet* just came along later and annihilated the corpse, but the whole crew was already dead by then. According to your spies, he waltzed right into *Shangdu*, stole something for Slavkov, and ambled right back out without anyone getting hurt. Somehow, Sokolov figured out we were there at *Svalbard* and those two managed to turn the entire game inside out on me."

She paused to think. And finished her own glass. She listened as Toov refilled it while her eyes stared off into deep space.

"Those two are as wily as eels," she decided. "And as dangerous. If Slavkov wants our help finding his ship, charge him extra."

"Even if it's personal, Turner?" Toov asked.

She nodded and hammered back the rest of the glass.

"I'd do the job for free," she replied in a cold voice. "But Slavkov dragged us into this mess, his personal vendetta, so he needs to pay us dearly for cleaning it up."

Toov studied her closely for a moment.

"Interesting assessment," he agreed. "And almost exactly what the Board concluded when he approached us for additional help. I want you to prepare your ship and your crew for an extended mission, Turner. We have spies out, looking for the Land Leviathan, and Navarre. I'm planning to send you in when we have a target."

Turner Kowalski smiled. She had never met Navarre personally, or known anyone who had. She had only been at the short end of his games.

She was looking forward to the opportunity to kill him.

Djamila found it interesting, just listening in as the conversations wound around her. Highly technical men and women, pushing the envelope, aware that they would only get one opportunity at the task in front of them.

She had nothing to do at this point, so she took up her usual station on *Hammerfield*'s bridge and knitted. This was a peace offering, of sorts, in gray and black twinned yarn. Extra fine material, with her smallest needles, so the going was slow, but the final product would be indistinguishable from something generated by an industrial machine.

The rest of the bridge was hyped, keyed up for the final assault that they were going to launch soon, but Djamila felt more like *Hammerfield* itself, calmly awaiting the countdown, clear out at the edge of the *Nidavellir* system.

Watching. Absorbing. Preparing.

At least *Hammerfield* would have something to do when they arrived. The only time Djamila would have any tasks at all would be if everything went desperately wrong and she ended up leading her teams against an enemy boarding action.

At which point, they were all likely dead, either way.

But the people around Djamila were still tuning things:

Javier, Zakhar, and Suvi here on the bridge; talking to Afia and her crew of engineers over there. Everything was almost ready.

Djamila had to send wanted her best people along with Afia, since the woman was going to be high on someone's kill list, when this was done. The initial support team had included Sascha, Hajna and Farouz, in case that team had to land on the planet and escape.

Logistics had prevented it, since they needed every available seat on the escape pod for engineers, and none of Djamila's people could be taught the necessary skills in the time available.

Hopefully, nothing would go wrong, and she would see everyone again in a few hours.

In her hands, two balls of very fine yarn slowly melted, feeding the pattern in her lap. Djamila had no way of knowing, short of asking outright, if Javier would recognize some of the patterns she was working into this sweater. Anyone outside of *Neu Berne* probably wouldn't but she also knew he had studied her culture, her past, at least enough to know which of her buttons to push, and how.

Back when they both pushed buttons.

It was a strange feeling, not constantly looking for ways to kill the man and make it look like an accident. Not wondering if Suvi would change her mind about killing Djamila. Or how Zakhar would react to a quiet knock at his door.

Djamila had decades to understand who she was turning into. And Javier to thank for it. Or blame, depending.

She smothered a smile before it erupted and lit up the whole bridge. Humming to herself would be even worse.

And yet.

She was still the *Ballerina of Death*. Still seven of the top ten scores on the combat range, although she suspected that Farouz could shorten that count, if he chose.

They had only been intimate once, she and Farouz. She had hoped for more, but the man brought his own sensibilities to the prospect of Operational Security. Djamila respected that.

And respected the promise, the fire, she saw in his eyes, that when this mission was over and they could relax, they could once again just be evil pirates roaming the spaceways and causing mischief.

So she knitted.

After Javier's sweater was done, something for Farouz would be next. She just wasn't sure what it would be. Or maybe she'd do something for Afia first, while she thought about what to do for this new man in her life.

A message pinged on her board, distracting her.

Javier.

Interesting, since he was seated all of eight meters away from her. He could had spoken aloud in a normal voice. Or simply gotten up and walked over.

She opened the message.

"*Morningstar Brigade?*" the message said.

Yes. Her old unit.

There was a picture attached, which she opened. It matched the symbol she had worked into the center of the sweater's chest in black and gray in her lap.

She smiled in spite of herself. Djamila would have thought that Suvi would be the only other person on this bridge that would recognize the design. And Javier hadn't gotten close while she was working, so he had to have been studying her from his usual distance.

It made her warm to think she still had that much effect on the man.

Rather than type, she just turned her head far enough to extend her smile to Javier. She nodded at his obvious confusion.

Javier did not speak. He typed instead.

"So who is this sweater for?" he pinged.

It was interesting how little emotional loading there was on such simple words. Coming out of his mouth, there would have been sarcasm, or *ennui*. Something.

This felt like simple curiosity. Which might be why he had chosen this method. They could be polite and friendly, without maintaining the outward aggression and friction that had framed their relationship for so many years.

Maybe he was finally growing up and acting like

management. After all, the horse might truly have learned to sing, given enough time.

Djamila bit her lip to stop from giggling at the image. Instead of speaking, she typed a message, and then looked up to see Javier's response.

"You," she volleyed back.

The shock on his face was like the best pudding for dessert, after the best steak imaginable.

After all, she did owe him, from way back.

Torturing Javier Aritza with kindness was probably going to be even better than killing him.

C OMMODORE WAS A COURTESY TITLE, rather than a rank. Senior captain on a station that did not warrant an admiral. Back in his line command days, being a commodore would mean commanding a small task force.

Captain Nguyên Ayokunle wasn't in command in the field anymore. He had gotten promoted about as far as he was ever going to, and was in charge of the military section at *Merankorr*, while he waited for his retirement in a few years.

It was a cushy job, but never that exciting. Part accountant. Part bureaucrat. Part spy. *Concord* Fleet Operations relied on him to wade through mountains of electronic paperwork, looking for trends, patterns, and issues, so they could be reconciled or deflected before they got too big to handle easily. He was good at what he did, and afraid that he was about to make a career-ending mistake.

That, or perhaps kill the man who had been his best friend once.

Yên sat in the Admiral's outer office and waited for that man. The space was comfortable, painted in a soft peach, with green carpet that looked vaguely grass-like. The couch he was on was designed to be relaxing, but not so much that you risked falling asleep. Two plants in pots that he couldn't identify, along with oil paintings that looked like pre-spaceflight seascapes.

Men trapped in storms. It was an interesting choice of decoration.

The inner door opened and a young lieutenant commander stepped out, looking for all the galaxy like a recruiting poster image. Short, dark hair. Chiseled features. Trim and athletic.

Probably the nephew of somebody well-connected that the admiral wanted to impress.

"Commodore?" the man said, coming more or less to attention. "The admiral will see you now, sir."

The young man gestured Yên to enter the room, and then closed the hatch behind him.

Inside, the peach and green theme continued. Similar artwork. More potted plants.

The only weird thing about the room was the enormous fish tank in one corner. Yên could smell the salt water from here, and see dozens of fish moving around in a space as big as three coffins stacked atop one another.

The admiral behind the desk was relatively new on this station. Physically average for size, height, and weight. At least for an admiral, where they tended to get squishy with rank. The man's skin was as pale as Yên's was dark. The only thing the men had in common was gone hair completely white, but neither man bald.

Yên hadn't had enough time around the man, past that, to really get a feel for him, but things were moving fast right now, and it couldn't wait.

"Commodore," Admiral Jameson Packard said in a gruff greeting. "Sit."

Yên did, trying to gauge the man's humor.

"I've read your report to Intelligence on the man called Sokolov," the admiral continued, focusing those eyes like angry emeralds on him. "How much of your conclusion is supported purely on facts, and how much on intuition?"

Yên licked his lips carefully.

"The raw findings are solidly empirical, sir," Yên said. "The vessel was close enough to us, for long enough, for good solid soundings to be made. Naval Estimates Board was able to match the hull with their records. She is definitely one of the last generation of *Neu Berne* galleons, built in the last five years of that war. We've narrowed it down to one of four hulls, but would need to get inside her to get a solid identification. Sokolov, or someone else, did some significant modifications later, possibly recently. Two of the main pulsars were upgraded to pulse cannons, and one was replaced with an ion pulsar. That would match our estimates of weapons taken off *Storm Gauntlet*, in her last known weapons configuration."

"What about torpedoes?" the admiral bored in.

"Unknown how many *Storm Gauntlet* had," Yên replied. "But other intelligence reports suggest that *Storm Gauntlet* fought a battle with a pirate vessel at *Svalbard* a year ago, and damaged that ship with them."

"And the information on…Sokolov?" Packard asked.

"I updated the files with what I knew, right up until the point he took his retirement and vanished seventeen years ago. Modern notes are from Naval Estimates Board's records of the organization he supposedly worked for, plus what the man told me himself when we spoke briefly here and aboard *Shangdu*."

"And the *Khatum of Altai* is definitely involved?" the admiral asked.

"By her own admission, Admiral," Yên agreed.

"Letters of Marque and Reprisal represent a dangerous escalation, Captain," Packard observed. "Especially in a warship of that magnitude. Doubly so in the wilderness, where there might not be any other vessels capable of stopping them."

"Aye, sir," Yên said. "However, Navarre's stated intent was to cripple Walvisbaai Industrial. *Salt the earth* were his actual words."

"And you wish to stop him?" Packard asked. "Or assist him?"

"Neither, Admiral," Yên admitted. "I take both men at face value that they will do one thing, and then get on with their lives. If I am right, we have the chance to hold some amount of leverage over the final outcome."

"With a Class II Warmaster, alone?" the admiral sneered.

"Human crewed vessels cannot navigate hyperspace as quickly as *Sentient* vessels can, Admiral," Yên responded. "I pushed as hard as I could to get here. *Concord Warship Meridian* could get us to *Nidavellir* fast enough, I think, to help pick up the pieces, if nothing else. Or stop them, if they decide to go completely rogue over an inhabited planet."

"With you as task force commander?" the admiral asked.

"I know the man, Admiral Packard," Yên said. "Knew him forty years ago. Maybe I can stop him, or something. And if not, I'd rather be the one to kill him, instead of sending someone else to handle the task."

Packard studied him for several seconds.

"Very well, Captain Ayokunle," the man said. "It's your reputation on the line, either way. I'll let you own this one. Prepare yourself for transit. Orders will be transmitted shortly."

Yên rose and saluted. He was more of a spy and a bureaucrat these days. It would be nice to get back in the saddle one last time.

BOOK TWENTY-SEVEN: NIDAVELLIR

Javier studied the boards in front of him. One last mission as the *Science Officer*, and then he might retire to the life of shipping magnate. Or chicken breeder. There was space down in one of the cargo decks, maybe all the way down on Seventeen, to install a much larger botany lab than he had brought from *Mielikki* to *Storm Gauntlet* to here. Maybe he could have a small petting zoo. How would the crew feel about fresh cream on a daily basis to go with fresh eggs?

Real, homemade cheese.

Tomorrow's problems.

Today, the mission that would cement his legend as the most famous, most dangerous pirate in the last millennium. Possibly the most wanted man in space.

Did he really want to make that big of a mark on history? Kill as many people as he might, if the morons over there got too wrapped up in their invulnerability?

Yeah, he did. Bullies just got on his nerves.

And, seriously, Valko Slavkov had just pushed all of his buttons.

The bridge was silent, almost a cathedral today. Or a tomb.

Everyone was poised. Engines had been tuned. Weapons loaded and aligned. Torpedo bays inspected. Crazed, lunatic, goofball *Sentience* about to pay back a small portion of her anger at having been trapped in that little survey probe for years.

Even Sykora had achieved a new level of calm.

Javier wasn't sure he wouldn't have preferred bitch-on-wheels Djamila to this new version that was turning into a butterfly before his eyes.

On his boards, live faces representing all the major players: Djamila, Piet, Mary-Elizabeth, Djamila, Suvi, Afia, Andreea, Zakhar.

The *Pirates*.

He had brought them here on the basis of his rage. Nothing more. Transcended slavery to become a leader they were about to follow into battle.

Zakhar was poised. Walvisbaai Industrial had killed *Storm Gauntlet*. That man's pride and joy. He was more than happy to return some element of favor today. *Angry Patriarch*.

Piet had spoken more words to the crew in the last six months than he had in the previous ten years, to hear the old-timers talk. And even started composing and performing music with Suvi. Weird.

Afia looked like a pixie grizzly bear. Petite. Serious. About to rip your throat out.

Mary-Elizabeth had a smile like she had just been offered an extra scoop of ice cream for her birthday. Considering that woman's calling in life, maybe there was some truth to it.

Djamila looked up from her knitting to smile. It wasn't warm. Not like before. Serious. Like she was prepared to open fire on everything that moved with pistols tucked into her bag. She probably was.

Andreea looked pensive and distracted, but she was an introvert's introvert, and looked like that anyways. Her greatest day was when every single generator and engine was running within one percent of optimal. Like today.

Javier met Suvi's eyes. She was still his oldest friend in the galaxy, barring two angry ex-wives and a host of siblings and cousins he hadn't spoken to in ten or twenty years.

She looked calm. Prepared. They had talked about

everything, starting with *Shangdu* and *Svalbard*, and coming up to the present. The Pleasure Dome. The Doomsday Vault. The Last Flagship. The War of the Pirate Clans.

Javier was sure those people over there approached all of this like accountants and bankers. That's what it was to most of them. Money and gross points. And Valko Slavkov was just a petulant, abrasive punk who bullied people. Javier had asked Behnam, and she hadn't been able to name anyone who truly liked the man.

They just feared his temper, magnified by his immense wealth. He was among the twenty wealthiest individuals in the galaxy by individual value.

Nobody had ever told that man *No*, and actually made it stick.

Javier wasn't sure this would do the job with that punk, but it would certainly *materially damage the future of Walvisbaai Industrial as a going concern*, which was how you got the attention of accountants and bankers. The quarterly report wouldn't be able to gloss this over.

Shareholders would take notice. Demand changes. Revenge was a losing proposition, except when someone fell into your hands and you could profitably sell them on the black market without much effort.

If nobody was willing to work with or for Slavkov, he would either be neutered, or have to spend monumental amounts of cash just to get anything done.

Victory, either way.

Suvi's face summed that up. She had run those numbers for him, working with one of the *Khatum*'s people, possibly Tömörbaatar. That man was more dangerous with a pen than a blade, although Javier wasn't willing to try his luck with either. Not with the man in the silly hat.

Suvi nodded, as if she could read his mind. Considering how much poker he had taught her over the years, she might be able to do just that.

Both of his ex-wives, Holly and Fryda, had always claimed with some truth, that Javier wasn't really that much deeper than a mud puddle. Even this was just a playground squabble, blown up all out of proportion by two men who wouldn't back down.

Javier nodded back and watched her smile reassuringly. Most of this would be in her hands, once they passed no-return. Mary-Elizabeth and Piet would provide expert assistance. Zakhar would command.

But Suvi would make or break the day. And the bad guys.

He wondered what outfit she was wearing in the privacy of her own cockpit. She had presented baseline Yeoman *Sentience* for this.

Javier knew better. She was too much of a goofball.

Still, time for business.

Javier turned and looked up at Zakhar, Zeus-like atop his mighty throne, lightning bolt in one hand.

"You wanna do this?" Javier asked in a slow, deep voice.

Zakhar wore a scowl that would frighten kittens.

"No," Captain Sokolov replied in a dark, ominous tone. "This one's yours, beginning to end. We're here because you gave us a reason to survive as a company. This is an ending, and hopefully a beginning. It should be your speech."

Javier nodded. About what he had expected. And simple truth.

Zakhar would have broken them up and sold the little strike corvette for scrap, without someplace better to go. Ridden off into the sunset, maybe with Djamila, maybe not.

Everyone else would have been put to shore, then frantically scrambled to find work, at a time when too many of them had prices on their heads in too many places. And possibly lawmen or assassins lurking in the shadows.

Where did that leave him? Four years ago, he had sworn to see every single one of these bastards hung from a high yardarm in low gravity.

And here he was, about to lead them into battle. Save them from a fate as bad as death.

Obviously, the gods had a very dark, bitter sense of humor.

Javier reached down and pressed a virtual button on his screen marked *Ship-wide Comm*.

He took a deep breath and let it go.

"The reasons we are here are legion," he began simply, listening to the words echo out over the big room as Suvi adjusted the feedback. "Not all of them are benign, as we are none of us angels."

Javier kept his face on Zakhar for now, watching the impact the words had on the man who might have been his slave-master, and eventually his partner. Tomorrow, perhaps, his friend.

"At the most basic, they tried to kill us," Javier continued. "Nothing more than that. Pissy, little punk throwing a temper tantrum because everything didn't go his way. So he hired those people across the way to kill us. That makes me angry."

Javier paused to let the energy build. In his own mind, they were already past no-return, but he needed to bring everyone with him. Convince them that this was a hill worth dying on.

"They would have killed you as well," he continued. "And without today, probably would have tried again and again until they eventually got lucky."

Deep breath. All those lessons in public speaking at *Bryce Academy*, back when he wanted to be an officer and gentleman when he grew up. If he had ever decided to grow up.

Maybe today was as good as any. Djamila could. Piet could. Even Zakhar could.

Maybe Javier Aritza could as well.

"You do not negotiate with bullies," he declared in a voice growing both louder and sharper, like a bastard sword clearing a scabbard for battle. "You push them back. And you do not do it just a little. Ladies and gentlemen, they started this. I intend to end it. Right here. Right now. We will make the galaxy a better place by destroying some of the worst elements around. Whatever else you must face your Creator bearing on your list of sins, remind Her that you were here today, and you did this thing."

Javier didn't bother looking at the rest of the bridge crew. He could already tell that everyone had stopped what they were doing to look over at him. On his boards, the little images were backs of heads, instead of faces.

All except Afia.

Javier focused his intent on that woman now. Felt his eyes grow slitted and fierce. She matched him, blow for blow.

"*Odysseus*," he commanded. "Make your jump."

Afia pressed a button on her command console and felt the little shiver of power that vibrated through the vessel's hull like a mild orgasm. So much power at her fingertips.

She had always been an engineering nerd. Quiet. Competent. Way more sociable than most. It had gotten her to *Meehu* with 'Mina, Piet, and Djamila. Given her the chance to shine in front of Javier, so that he pulled her into the big adventures, like *Hammerfield*.

Put her here, now. Commanding the prize crew of engineers and the stolen freighter renamed *Odysseus*, now departing on her terminal mission.

The stars blinked out, leaving all screens a gray fuzz of static in the space between universes.

Afia looked around the big, friendly bridge one last time from her awesome vantage in the captain's chair. It was kinda seductive, sitting here. She might have to think about it, one of these days. Javier had started out as an engineer, and he could be a pretty good commander.

Maybe the universe was just waiting for Afia Burakgazi to decide to join those ranks.

She pressed the ship-wide button.

"All hands," she ordered in a calm voice that wanted to rage over into giggles. "Final jump initiated. Prepare for scuttling charges and the order to evacuate."

She closed the comm before the evil laughter in her belly snuck out.

So much power. It might be Javier's plan. And Suvi's execution. But Afia was going down in history as the woman who pulled it off.

Aft, eight men and women would be frantically pulling arming pins and unlocking explosive charges, made awkward by the combat suits they were wearing. Afia had decreed that nobody was going into this mission wearing only skinsuits. The extra few seconds were worth the protection, if something went wrong.

On a secondary board, lights began to turn blue. Some had been green, others red. Blue mean active and ready for her to give the order.

"Ilan," she barked into the comm. "One-Three-One just went from green to black. Check it out. I need that circuit."

"On it," the man called back.

Five years ago, that landsman would have been hard pressed to get his shoes on the correct feet. Today, he was a First-Rank Machinist. Would have been on an officer track if he had the slightest interest. But he was happier tinkering.

Afia was fine with that.

The schedule had squishiness built in. Javier and Suvi had been a stickler for the fact that friction was going to come up at the wrong moment.

Like now.

One-Three-One controlled the whole port/aft charge. Without that one, there was a serious risk that the jack-knobs on the station could knock *Odysseus* off-course safely.

Once they figured out that she was intent on ramming them.

Boy, weren't they going to be in for a shock.

The lifeboat icon went light blue on her board. Everyone aboard except her and Ilan.

"Ilan?" she yelled into the comm.

The light had briefly flickered to green, then red, then blue, then black again.

"I've got a short somewhere," he called back.

"Well, you're out of time to fix it," Afia replied.

"I can do this!" he cried.

She reached up to the extra rocker switch that had been hard-wired onto the console and flipped the protective cover up. Underneath, a lovely pin-switch in the up position.

It took a little effort to break the switch free and snap it down. You had to have *intent*.

Immediately, the lights everywhere got a red tinge. Suvi's recorded voice emerged from every speaker on every deck. Loud enough that you didn't miss it.

"Warning," she said in a big, soothing voice, like mom trying to get your butt out of bed on a Saturday. "Emergency charges activated. Self-destruction in five minutes and counting. All hands abandon ship."

Afia took an extra second to lock her board. The chances of someone getting in here and disarming it were next to nil, but why make it any easier than she had to?

Out the hatch, down the stairs, across the beam of the ship to the corner. She had the longest run to get to the lifeboat, located aft where everyone else was working. She chose Port just to make sure Ilan got his ass going and didn't wait too long.

They weren't about to prevent the lifeboat's automated systems from taking off in four minutes. If he wasn't aboard, there were pods, but the chances of capture by really mad people went off the charts if that happened.

Afia was moving at a good jog, but she could see Ilan's butt sticking out of a wall panel, one leg in the air like a dog.

"Out of time, Sailor," she yelled as she got closer. "Leave it and go."

"I can fix it," his muffled voice echoed weirdly up the hall.

Worst part? He probably could, given another ten minutes. The boy had mad skills, but no sense of time.

Afia slowed to a walk as she got close.

"Now, Ilan," she ordered.

Just to make sure, she grabbed the leg in the air and pulled him by the ankle.

Ilan scrambled angrily to his feet and lurked over her.

"Damn it, Afia!" he raged. "I almost had it."

She had never seen him this mad. Up close, she came up to about his collar bone, and massed at least a third less. And there was murder in his eyes as he took a half step towards her.

"I gave you an order, Sailor," she fired back, almost growling. It was a tone Djamila had taught her. "Leave it. Right now. Move."

Some measure of sanity snapped back into those brown eyes. Ilan came back to himself.

"Yes, sir," he said in a quieter tone.

Rather than chance it, Afia grabbed him by the arm and physically propelled him down the hallway ahead of her. If one charge sequence failed, she might just order Suvi to fire on the hulk.

A good, hard jolt might set it off.

They were only going to get one chance at this, and there had been no way to do a dress-rehearsal.

Ilan went through the last hatch, onto the flight deck, two steps ahead of her. He threw himself into the lifeboat without breaking stride and fell into the open seat on the right.

Afia took the seat on the left and counted noses.

Everyone here. Time to go.

She opened the emergency comm line.

"*Excalibur*, this is *Odysseus*," she said, panting with the exertion. "Launching now."

And she pressed the big, red button in the middle of the console.

An emergency tone sounded as the hatch slid shut and locked itself in place. The screen counted down from ten.

At ZERO, it fired them into deep space at four times the force of gravity.

On the screen, the wall of metal behind her quickly turned into a ship, rapidly receding as she raced away.

About the time Afia finally caught her breath, Afia's first independent command died in fire.

PART THREE

Suvi took a deep breath.

Imagined a deep breath. Whatever electronic beings did to find their equilibrium and focus as the shit was about to get very nasty outside.

She still had the occasional twinge about not following through on Javier's original plan to see all the pirates in the galaxy hung from yardarms, but most of these people had turned out to be pretty okay folks.

Even the dragon lady was kinda nice, which was all levels of weird.

Suvi decided that she should blame Zakhar for everything. It made a nice symmetry, all in all. Especially the bits nobody had told Javier about.

Yet.

Outside, the warm whisper of solar wind on her skin, muted as she dropped out of jump with her shields already at max setting and every weapons system on-line and armed. Mary-Elizabeth tuning firing solutions was kinda like being tickled by goldfish.

Suvi looked around and launched a pair of probes into orbit in both directions. She locked onto them with tight-beam communications lasers. She would need eyes to see the station itself as *Odysseus* caught fire in front of her, a flaming shield interposed between Suvi's bow and *Walvisbaai Industrial Platform Number One.*

The object of today's lesson.

Ahead of her, below her, the planet *Nidavellir*, the big green and blue planet that apparently served as a mostly empty hinterland to feed and entertain the big-wigs of the galactic corporate conglomerate generally known as Walvisbaai Industrial. She counted seventeen other major stations in orbit and visible at present, with eleven more behind the curve of the planet, one way or the other.

Number One was the only one she really cared about.

Piet started tickling her too, but he had music in mind, so she listened.

Down and in. Soften the drive three percent to let raw inertia handle the orbital insertion instead of using thrusters to hold her space.

Piet really was a master of this sort of thing. She could learn from the best.

Around her, the comm channels went into total freakout mode as Slavkov's transport imploded and started to disintegrate into big, chewy chunks. Most people probably assumed a complete systems failure coming out of jump that had led to a catastrophic event.

'Cept it t'wer'n't no accident.

Not with a capital-class warship of unknown provenance suddenly appearing as well, conveniently tucked in behind the slowly-spreading wreckage in such a way that the big guns on the station were blocked and would have to fire through it to get to her.

Whoops.

Suvi displayed a full system schema as she scanned every ship in orbit. She knew Piet, Mary-Elizabeth, and Zakhar were following every shift, every twitch. A few others had the same display on their screens, mostly as background. Most people seemed to be watching a live feed of *Odysseus* coming apart. Way more interesting.

She decided to add to the chaos. The longer it took people to figure this out, the worse the damage was likely to be.

"Mayday," she called in her best imitation of panic. "Transport *Odysseus* has suffered a total failure. Any vessels within range please assist."

For fun, she threw that on a loop and used her main transmitter to override every damned signal she could find, except for one station broadcasting classical music, oboe concertos right now, way down at the quiet, lonely end of the dial. She liked their choice of programming today. Let them be.

Technically, this was piracy of the worst kind. Abraam Tamaz and his Q-ship *Salekhard* had done this sort of thing, but they did it to lure in victims. That was why Javier had killed him.

One of the reasons.

Today, Suvi just wanted everybody confused as hell. Pretty soon, someone would catch on that this was an attack and come after her, but there was nobody wearing big-girl panties on the other side except the station itself. And he was about to be in all sorts of trouble.

Let's see. There, there, and…Oh? Who's this? Gosh, you picked a bad day to be on the wrong side of the tracks, Ajax.

Suvi highlighted a signal on Zakhar's board and added transponder information. She added Mary-Elizabeth and Piet into the mix a second later.

Mary-Elizabeth Suzuki, gunner, still had choice things to say about those people.

"Captain," Suvi said out loud, just to make sure he was paying attention. "I have identified the Raider-class heavy frigate *Ajax*, just breaking orbit and headed this way. Orders?"

"Ignore her," Zakhar said, surprising Suvi. "Mary-Elizabeth, add a firing solution to overload *Ajax* with four torpedoes when she decides to come after us. Otherwise, Kowalski's not going to know it's us until much later. Stay on topic here, please."

Huh.

Actually, that made sense. Turner Kowalski's last

encounter with this crew had been when she nearly killed them all aboard the strike corvette *Storm Gauntlet*, almost a year ago.

"Roger that," Mary-Elizabeth muttered through gritted teeth.

Suvi could tell the gunner felt the same way about the need to stomp the little ship like an empty tin can. Maybe they'd get lucky today.

"*Excalibur*, this is *Nidavellir* Orbital Control," a voice finally came in. Somebody had brought an entire generator inline, just to punch through her hash of static and random music videos. "Stand down. This is a controlled sector. Acknowledge and begin to decelerate or we will open fire."

Not bad. Only took them five minutes to decide maybe they were facing a raid and not a rescue. Afia was nearly a third of the way across the gap, and just turning over to decelerate. She'd be safely aboard in seven minutes, and then the crazy dancing could begin.

It was kinda like watching things through a periscope, having those probes out either direction around the flaming mess of the transport's slowly-diverging pieces. She could see ships suddenly light their engines and come out to help.

'Fox-babe in the henhouse' time.

The other two signals she wanted to play with had lit their thrusters the moment *Odysseus* had dropped into real space. They were coming out to play, and had brought their shields up and started scanning hard.

But they still thought they were rescuing the crew of the transport.

Suvi had been unable to find any other name for them besides Escort Red and Escort Blue, which just went to show you how boring and predictable some people were. She would have called them Stan and Ollie, just for the hell of it.

Nobody but a librarian was going to get the joke, anyway.

Ahead of her, something was going wrong with *Odysseus*. Not horrible bad, but it looked like a failure of the detonation sequence she had programmed. Damned barge should have turned into about six big pieces and a couple dozen smaller ones, but two of them hadn't spalled off.

Technically, she wasn't supposed to engage on her own. *Concord* law was very specific about *Sentient* beings using weapons on organics.

Big no-no.

She lined up one of the turrets, accounted for off-set and tumble, and changed the targeting screen Mary-Elizabeth was using to a much tighter focus.

"Captain," Suvi began. "There appears to have been a problem with scuttling the freighter. Request permission to fire into the hulk to set off the remaining charges."

Because everyone had a multi-screen edge on their monitors, all faces were in front of you at all times when you were an organic. Suvi had everyone projected at real height in a full three dimensions, standing around her little cockpit.

As fast as she processed, there were occasionally hours of downtime for her between sentences. Especially when a human had to react to something new.

Ajax was moving in the right direction to open fire shortly. *Stan* and *Ollie* had taken tighter tracks that would get them in a position to drop EVA teams and rescue lifepods blasting for the surface.

Sokolov still moved like a *Concord* captain. It was nice, pretending to be back in the fleet again.

"Kill it," he ordered in a flat tone. "Then cycle forward and begin putting shots through the wreckage like icepicks. Bring his shields down, but ignore him except to counter-battery weapon mounts as they clear."

"Roger that, sir," Suvi replied, all giddy in her girly bits as Mary-Elizabeth pushed the big, red button on her main screen.

Suvi fired three quick shots into the ass end of *Odysseus* as it tumbled.

Boom.

Six ball in the corner pocket. Eleven in the side. Draw for the next shot with a little of Piet's English.

She could get the taste for being a bad-ass warship, working with these folks. There was more than geometry to this sort of thing, apparently. Piet and Mary-Elizabeth had art.

Ajax was clear of the flames. Suvi shifted energy to those shields, since there was nobody behind her right now.

A shot flashed out. Miss by a mile.

Except.

Crap.

That nearly got Afia's lifeboat.

No. Did. Just kissed it, which was pretty good shooting at this range. The little boat was starting to shed pieces as it turned over. Looked like it was losing control and beginning to tumble.

Suvi saw red. Or finally understood the human term.

She wanted blood. Turner Kowalski's.

Torpedoes were locked on different targets and it would take too long to get one over there anyway. She snapped the ion pulsar around by overloading the drive motors hard enough that they would need to be repaired later.

Lined that bitch up.

The lock-outs on the weapons were designed to keep it from overloading by firing too rapidly. Suvi cut them out of the circuit and shifted all five spare generators into the weapons array.

The result wasn't a firehose, but the shots were fast enough that a human would barely see them. Woodpecker on speed.

Suvi opened a laser comm to Ajax as the ship went all St. Elmo's fire.

"Captain Kowalski, and crew of the vessel *Ajax*, this is Suvi, the *Sentience-in-Residence* aboard the galleon *Excalibur*," she ground the words out in a tone Javier might have used today. "If you ever fire on a lifeboat again, I will shatter your vessel with pulse fire and torpedoes, and then hunt down every lifepod and emergency suit you launch until there are no possible survivors. I don't care if you understand. This was your only warning."

Not like *Ajax* was going to do anything for the next minute or three. Even a warship like that needed to bleed the overload off into batteries before things started behaving. Especially with what she had just done to them.

Mary-Elizabeth apparently agreed. Suvi felt the big Pulse Cannon turret lining up, let it, felt the gunner's anger in the targeting reticule.

Mary-Elizabeth fired the weapon once. It was a masterful display, as *Ajax*'s shields just barely held under the hammering assault.

The whole ventral line of pulse turrets was pretty much inline as well. Mary-Elizabeth shifted the first weapon left. Not much, just a drift. The kind of thing that would leave a scratch down the side of a flitter in a parking lot.

She fired. Suvi made a note of the sequence, because that was why M-E got paid the big bucks.

The shot passed through the tissue-paper leftovers of *Ajax*'s aft shields and spalled a huge chunk of metal off a corner. Didn't penetrate all that deeply, but Suvi watched metal sublime under the intense heat. A cloud of plasma erupted.

First Law of Thermodynamics. Energy can be transformed from one form into another, but must be conserved.

In this case, *Ajax* began to pitch, roll, and yaw as the glancing blow turned into a cloud of vaporized metal racing away from the hull, pushing hard the other direction and imparting spin.

Kowalski was going to be a while getting that under control, even after she got all the ionization cleared.

Suvi looked up, but Piet and Mary-Elizabeth had things under control. The galleon was generally sheltered from the shit-storm of fire erupting out of the station.

Contrary to all Suvi's favorite video games, ships in combat rarely exploded, except when you managed to blow engineering apart just right. Fighting with pulsars was frequently like stabbing someone to death with icepicks. And those morons on the station were trying to blow apart chunks of *Odysseus* as they tumbled closer and closer.

"*Hammerfield*, I am declaring an emergency."

The words froze Suvi's soul.

Machinist Ilan Yu. In the lifeboat. On the comm.

Instead of Afia.

Very, very, very not good.

Suvi replayed the signal on the bridge speakers as she spoke.

"Go ahead, Ilan," she said, trying to keep her voice calm.

Damn it, electronic beings weren't supposed to act emotional. That was a chemical thing. An organic thing.

But these were her friends.

"The lifeboat has suffered catastrophic failure," he said in a calmer voice than she could manage right now. "Control systems are compromised and we will miss rendezvous. Ship is in the process of coming apart and I have casualties."

Casualties. Friends hurt, maybe dying. Maybe already dead.

Suvi ground her teeth.

"Suvi, lock out the torpedoes," Zakhar barked in a voice that sounded remarkably like Doom itself. "Now."

Suvi did. Orders were orders and that programming went bone deep.

Mary-Elizabeth uttered a string of curses as she hammered the launch button with her fist a second time.

Oh.

M-E had been about to annihilate *Ajax*. Six torpedoes at an ionized destroyer would probably actually be enough to blow the little ship into spare parts and rabbit kibble.

"Why?" Mary-Elizabeth growled, but Zakhar wasn't having it.

Suvi was pretty sure she had never seen the man angry.

Until now.

"Gunner," he said in a low, sepulchral tone. "I gave you an order to ignore *Ajax*. Begin your firing sequence on station with torpedoes. You will thread the shots through the wreckage slowly enough that they can be engaged and possibly stopped by defensive fire. *Am I clear?*"

Mary-Elizabeth gulped at the calm threat under those words.

Hell, Suvi gulped, but she unlocked the woman's firing screen as M-E nodded and began lining things up for drift and cover.

Suvi kinda sat back and watched. *Ajax* was neutralized. Piet and Mary-Elizabeth were murmuring targeting solutions data back and forth.

Zakhar looked like Death come for all their souls right now.

"Javier, Djamila," he ordered in a calm tone. "Take charge of the rescue. Del's already green on the boards."

Djamila had stashed her knitting in a bag on the floor. Suvi saw her nod once at Javier, silently, and then both of them began to run for the main hatch. Suvi tripped it open so they didn't have to break stride, and then turned her attention back to the battle raging in space around her.

Pretty soon, *Stan* and *Ollie* would have to come out to play. And *Ajax* would recover. And the boys on the station would figure out how to arc torpedoes ballistically to engage her, if they couldn't just pound their way through the meteor swarm threatening their front door.

Then things would get interesting.

Djamila knew a moment of polite surprise as she realized Javier was matching her stride for stride down the long hallway aft from the bridge. She stretched her legs and pushed, but didn't open that much of a lead on the man.

He must be in better shape than he used to be. Or he was that angry. There was always that.

Del was parked in the upper flight bay on Deck Seven, so they only had to pound down three flights of stairs. She made good time by going down three steps at a time.

Javier appeared to be hitting four. Hopefully, he knew his own limitations well enough to not take her out if he lost control.

Suvi was obviously watching them on internal monitors, because she was clearing hatches well enough ahead of them that Djamila never had to break stride as she ran.

Flight Deck.

Hajna and Sascha were already there, just boarding the Assault Shuttle as Djamila came into sight. Both women held up white duffle bags as a signal, so Djamila continued to run. The pathfinders had already grabbed emergency suits for both of her and Javier, already sized, so they could board and get into gear as Del broke loose into deep space.

She made the hatch with Javier breathing hard, right behind her. Since this was Del's deck, she grabbed an iron rod set into a bulkhead for exactly this purpose, let her momentum swing her out of the way, and grabbed Javier with her other hand.

Hajna was already palming the hatch closed.

"Del," Hajna called. "All aboard. Launch when ready."

"All hands, brace for emergency maneuvers," the calm, old curmudgeon called back.

Djamila pulled Javier close, hugging him with the bar between them.

He started to resist, before he realized what she was doing, and then wrapped his arms around her hips.

Sascha was already strapped in. Hajna grabbed the bar on the other side.

Djamila's only warning was the shuttle kipping up on her toes, like a raptor about to grab sky. A moment of queasiness as the shuttle started to move laterally, like pork fat dancing across a hot grill. Surge of pure power as Del went through the lockshield at a speed not recommended by either manufacturers.

"Thank you," Javier said as he unburied his nose from between her breasts, turned, and grabbed the bag Sascha was pressing in his direction.

Djamila actually felt a blush threaten, but she crushed it before it ever got anywhere. She slid into the seat next to Hajna and began stripping layers.

Emergency EVA meant the hard-suits. For anything less, she would have trusted her skills in zero grav and a skinsuit, even with the other three maneuvering around her.

The lifeboat had engineers who would be as graceful as pigs on ice. Plus there were casualties.

Like all things between them, it turned into a race with Javier to see who could get naked and suited up faster. She had more length, but he had all the complicated plumbing attachments that came with being a boy.

Without looking at a slow motion replay, she would call it a draw, as both helmets snapped shut almost simultaneously.

"Cargo deck, we have matched speed with the lifeboat," Del

called over the radios. "She is tumbling slowly forward, somewhat aft relative off our starboard wing. I can see interior bulkheads through gaps, but she appears to be mostly intact. Sykora, you have the deck."

"Flight deck," she called back over the radio as everyone's external lights went green. "Begin depressurizing."

Lights went red and strobing. Djamila hadn't bothered turning on the external microphones, but she knew that alarms were busy warning everyone that this space would shortly be in death pressure.

The easiest way to do this was to just seal Del up in his little cockpit and open everything else.

Del had shut down the gravplates at the same time as the life support, so she got her feet under her and propelled herself softly to an arms locker tucked into one bulkhead. Inside, she found the springbolt and cable for transitioning between vessels that didn't have compatible airlocks. Or were tumbling too much to mate.

Or were trying hard not to be boarded by pirates. Not that something so banal had ever stopped her.

She grabbed what she needed, closed up the panel, and flew back across the space to where Sascha was just starting to open the landing ramp, letting in darkness. The sun was to her right and forward, so she would mostly be working in shadow here.

"Del," she called on the comm. "Nail them with spotlights, please."

"Already on, Djamila," he responded.

Good thing about working with Delridge Smith. He had seen it all, done it all. Calmest pilot she had ever flown with. One of the most professional, as well.

Djamila found the staple on the sidewall and attached one end of the line spool, as well as her safety line. Around her, the other three did the same.

She leaned out and turned to the left.

Del must be feeling cocky, or he was concerned about the casualties. The lifeboat was all of thirty meters away. She could have thrown a line to them and hit the hatch on her first try, eight times in ten.

Still, take no chances.

Djamila checked the springbolt, attached the weapon's harpoon line, and fired it across the small gap, patiently waiting as the line unspooled and the magnetic tip locked home.

She detached the spool from the weapon and flipped the switch to draw the line tight. Both ends had swivels, and the line itself could stretch under tension, plus the spool would feed extra line under torque. If this was going to take more than fifteen minutes, the tumbling might be a problem, but she doubted that would be the deciding issue today.

One quick glance to the right. *Hammerfield* in the distance, receding slowly as she closed on the station, hidden behind a small sea of big chunks of Slavkov's ship, blasted into pieces.

The steel fragments still had mass and momentum. Somebody aboard the station had finally figured that out and stopped trying to hit *Hammerfield*. Instead, the locals were pouring everything they had into the big, metal sections tumbling towards them inexorably.

Hammerfield was firing individual torpedoes on a slow metronome. Just enough to distract, and maybe strike home.

Djamila had seen the calculations done by Javier, Suvi, and Afia. The chances of the defenders succeeding, once the freighter had come apart and started to fall, were so low as to be irrelevant. Impact was assured at this point.

Good thing she shared the anger at Walvisbaai. What was it Javier had said?

Your Honor, they needed killing.

Yes. Yes, they did.

And if Afia was badly hurt, she might do it with her hands.

Back to the tiny ship.

Ilan Yu, or someone, was absolutely on the ball. She could see several people in suits working to attach safety lines to the connecting line so they could pull themselves over to the shuttle.

"Del, this is Ilan," the man's calm voice came over the radio.

It even sounded lower. More serious. "Seven mobile and headed your direction. I need assistance here. Afia's hurt and I can't transport her myself."

"Yu, this is Sykora," she said. "Stand by. My team will be there shortly."

"Roger that," he replied.

She felt someone grab her by the arm and swing her around. Javier touched faceplates, rather than call on the radio, so he wanted a private conversation.

"Free sail it?" he asked.

She glanced back around. Thirty meters? Relative zero motion? Time-sensitive?

She nodded and signaled the other two women what she was about to do.

Two steps and she was diving into eternity. Softly, without the surge of gravity she got when she did this off a ten-meter platform, but the physics were the same.

Turn over midway by piking, folding, and snapping. Fall feet-first, legs slightly spread, knees loose, grapple magnets activated.

Contact with inertia. She knelt and put a hand down for a perfect, three-point landing.

Javier had apparently been a step behind her again. And practicing. He landed well enough for someone who wasn't trained for combat insertions. Sascha and Hajna landed like mermaids.

Djamila waited for the last of the engineers to clear the hatch and begin their slow waddle-crawl over to Del and the shuttle, hand over hand and losing their local vertical as they spiraled. As long as the safety lines held, they would be fine. And she could always send one of the pathfinders after a stray duckling.

Djamila climbed in first.

Blood in zero gravity did strange things. Globules would achieve perfect stasis until they touched something, like bubbles. If it was cold enough, they would turn to ice drops first. If not, they might flatten out like pancakes.

The interior of the lifeboat was still mostly white, with only a few blotches of red forever frozen to the bulkhead.

Ilan was standing in the center of the small space, obviously locked down with magnets.

From the size alone, Djamila could have known it was Afia held to the side wall with engineer's tape. And partly mummified in it, as well. Her external monitors showed that she was still alive, but in very bad shape.

Djamila turned back to the machinist, and realized the right arm of his spacesuit was covered in blood nearly to the shoulder. More was splattered on his chest and faceplate, but just the sort of effect you got from someone bleeding on you in space.

"What happened?" she asked simply.

"Damage penetrated the interior of the vessel," Ilan fired off the words like an engineering report. "Everyone took some level of impact, but the armor on the suits stopped all of it except two easily-patched holes. A larger piece of shrapnel came loose from a wall and penetrated Afia's suit."

She indicated his arm silently.

"It was necessary to cut open her suit in death pressure," Ilan said calmly. "I removed the metal shard from the wound, taped up the wound as best I could, and then sealed her suit up with the tape as well. She's slowly leaking atmosphere, but I have a spare bottle of air handy and she will not need to swap out for at least sixteen minutes at her current rate of loss. I have her sedated now, but she will need surgery quickly to handle the damage to her abdomen."

Djamila nodded sagely.

Ilan Yu had been a complete waste of time and atmosphere when he first came aboard *Storm Gauntlet*. Aritza, with almost no redeeming qualities. A fuck-up they only kept because there were so few people they could recruit in those days and the man had at least been willing to try.

Djamila had been the one that suggested pairing him with the science officer when Aritza first came aboard, to see if it would do any good.

That action had probably already saved Afia's life today.

She barely recognized the man standing in front of her now.

Somebody growled quietly over the comm. It might have been Javier. Or maybe her.

Medical evac in this situation was actually pretty easy. The hardest part was always wrestling an immobile body without any friction or gravity against which to push.

Fortunately, Djamila Sykora was two hundred and eleven centimeters tall. That sort of reach let her do things the shorter people around her could not.

"Sascha and Hajna lead," she ordered. "Javier last. Ilan, stay close to me with your gear and spare bottle."

Quick assents. Professionals in a life and death situation.

Djamila reached down and pulled a knife from the outside belt. Engineer's tape could hold almost anything, but was designed to be easily cut. All the strength was in the adhesive, rather than the fabric that made it up.

She sliced Afia free, put away the knife, and grabbed the tiny woman with her left arm. The hatch was a stride away.

The two pathfinders were outside, holding the connecting cord, but had not attached safety lines, understanding that they might have to throw themselves one way or the other on short notice. Magnets alone held them in place.

Good.

Djamila watched the last of the slow engineers climb onto Del's deck and disappear from sight.

There were two ways to do this. Three if she followed the actual rules and attached her harness to the safety line, Afia's harness to her, and maintained complete control over all facets of motion at all times.

Time was critical.

"Sascha, go long," she called on the comm.

The pathfinder immediately launched herself up the line towards the shuttle. Djamila waited a moment and then thrust against the doorway, awkward with the added weight and slowly spinning, like a bullet leaving a barrel.

It would be better to get aboard the shuttle quickly.

Anything she did now could be fixed by the medbot on the ship. She just had to get there alive.

The landing ramp was like the mouth of a whale, intent on swallowing Djamila as prey.

Sascha had reached the far end of the line, grabbed on to stop, and spun. She reached out a hand, but Djamila was moving too fast to grab. All she did was knock Djamila off-center and start all three of them tumbling.

Djamila saw the bulkhead coming up, too fast to do anything about it. She thrust Afia away from her, backwards so the woman would not slam into it as hard as Djamila was about to. The extra inertia turned Djamila over even faster, and sped her up.

She slammed into the metal wall hard enough that it drove all the air out of her lungs. Stars circled in her vision. Bells began to ring from a distant church steeple.

Arms grabbed her, kept her from bouncing any more.

"Del," someone's voice called. "Seal her up."

Djamila wasn't sure which way up was, until the gravplates started to activate, slowly dragging her down to floor.

Someone was holding her in their lap like a child, but she was in no condition to actually move or resist. Whoever it was had pulled her into a seat and was buckling her in.

She was conscious. That was about it. Concussions were always a bitch.

The other faceplate looked down, brought her eyes into focus enough to see what was going in here.

Javier.

Huh.

He reached up and keyed her external medical override.

A hiss of something. Coldness on her neck.

Darkness.

PART FIVE

Zakhar studied a three-dimensional display of the battle, projected into the air in front of him in a space a meter across. *Hammerfield*'s gear was just so much better than *Storm Gauntlet* that it wasn't a fair comparison.

Mary-Elizabeth had been firing torpedoes like a drunk woodpecker. One here. One there. Goading the station into firing on *Hammerfield* and not the doomed steel avalanche coming at them.

He checked the weapon boards, just to be sure. Four torpedoes still locked hard on *Ajax*, just waiting for him to unlock them and let her kill Turner Kowalski. He considered it. The pirate was only now beginning to get her spin righted. Mary-Elizabeth might have done more damage to *Ajax*'s engines than she had planned with that one shot.

Or not. Mary-Elizabeth was that good.

Blue and *Red* were trying to coordinate rushing him, but they had a serious disadvantage right now, being below him in the gravity well, and unwilling to take on a cruiser big enough that he could have parked either of them in a cargo bay if he captured them.

And they were barely armed, compared to the big killer whale come for their little tuna souls.

The few shots they had attempted in his direction had barely licked his shields. He hadn't even bothered to have either of the armed women destroy them.

With Javier EVA, Tobias Gibney had taken over the science officer station. After this battle, Zakhar just needed to kick Javier off the bridge entirely. Gibney was good enough to do the job these days, and it wasn't like Aritza would be going anywhere.

"Science Officer," Zakhar barked in a tone that made most of the bridge twitch. "What is the status of the station's shield?"

Gibney double-checked before speaking. Another lesson he had learned from Javier.

"Below critical threshold, sir," Gibney replied quietly.

He did everything quietly. After three years aboard, Zakhar knew almost nothing about the man, except which planets he absolutely refused to ever take liberty on. And it was a weird list.

"Suvi," Zakhar continued. "We've got a few moments. Please rerun your calculations and confirm."

"Roger that, Captain," the woman said.

"Mary-Elizabeth," Zakhar made sure his voice sounded like a hammer driving nails into wood.

The pause was long enough that she turned to look at him, perhaps a shade sheepishly. She had let her emotions get the better of her. And her excitement.

"You will fire a single shot across *Ajax*'s bow," he ordered quietly. "And miss. This has gone on far enough."

"Yes, sir," the gunner replied in a quiet voice.

"Captain, calculations are confirmed," Suvi came back a moment later. "Three major pieces will definitely impact the station on their present course, as will a little less than half of all remaining shrapnel pieces."

"Gunner, you may fire when ready," Zakhar concluded.

"Firing one," Mary-Elizabeth called to the room.

On his boards, Zakhar watched the shot safely disappear into space.

"Bousaid, open a general comm," Zakhar said in a deep, angry voice. "Suvi, override all channels."

Zakhar watched his aide push a set of buttons on his board before turning and nodding.

"*Nidavellir* Orbital Control, this is the private service galleon *Excalibur*," Zakhar said quietly. "*Walvisbaai Industrial Platform Number One* is going to be destroyed by orbital collision. There is nothing anybody can do to stop it at this time. Captain Navarre feels that he has made his point, and we will be departing immediately. This is now a rescue operation on your part. We will not participate, but we will also not hinder it. If anyone fires on *Excalibur* after this message, I will rethink my decision."

Zakhar closed the channel and took a deep breath.

"Kibwe, put that on loop," he ordered.

It wasn't salting the earth. While some of these pieces, both the freighter and chunks bitten off the station, were large enough to survive re-entry, none of them were going to do much damage on the ground except for anyone unfortunate enough to be under them. And it was a sparsely-populated planet to begin with, or Zakhar would have never gone along with this plan.

This was just a reminder to Walvisbaai that taking Slavkov's money to kill Captain Navarre and Captain Sokolov came with consequences.

And things could have been much, much worse. There would be the inevitable casualties from a mass exodus in lifeboats under emergency conditions like this. Plus all the crap floating in near orbit, pieces blown off the station by Mary-Elizabeth's gunnery or shards of the Land Leviathan demanding right of way.

Zakhar figured he would be responsible for killing scores today, instead of thousands. He could live with that.

As Captain Navarre was famed for quoting, they were only killing pirates.

It was too bad there was nobody out there wealthy enough to hire him and Suvi to kill pirates for a living.

Maybe then he could atone for some of the terrible things he had done over the last decade.

And sleep at night.

On his boards, a simple green light appeared under the heading *Nidavellir* Orbital Control. They were apparently willing to accept the peace offering. Someone over there had probably done the same math and come to the same conclusion.

There was embarrassed, and there was suicidal. Pick your poison.

Ajax sheared off as well, choosing to abruptly go nose down into the gravity well with a hard turn on her gyros and a red-line on the engines. Even Turner wasn't that stupid, apparently.

"Piet, take us out," Zakhar said in a conversational tone.

Things were getting better. He was going to get out of this one alive.

A vessel as large as a First-Rate-Galleon had an over-abundance of power for her mass. That meant that the gravplates never flickered under combat conditions, like they occasionally had done back on *Storm Gauntlet*.

What happened next wasn't a flicker so much as a jolt.

"Bridge crew," Suvi called in a hard voice. "Enemy warship coming out of jump. Stand by for combat."

Because he still had everything already projected, Zakhar saw the dot appear. He felt the entire hull rumble underneath him as every gun turret moved at the same time. And all the shields forward suddenly got reinforced as Suvi pushed everything to red.

The transponder signal came up quickly. Faster than Gibney would have been able to locate it, but Suvi was a *Sentient* warship, and working at her own speed.

And hell, she might know the fellow.

Because that was a *Concord* ship over there. A *Class II Warmaster*. A ship more than capable of taking on *Hammerfield* on even terms, even before the mild damage and wear-and-tear from a one-sided orbital battle.

Things had just gotten bad.

PART SIX

Suvi didn't think most humans had ever really wrapped their heads around what it meant that with this hardware she thought twenty-one THOUSAND times faster than they did. Or that she could do ten different things, with ten different sets of hands, simultaneously, and never drop an egg while juggling.

This was a battle. The first she had gotten to fight since she had been de-commissioned out of *Concord* service twenty years ago. And Suvi was in a dedicated warship, built by the kind of crazed warrior culture that turned out people like Djamila Sykora on a regular basis.

Power.

She was *Athena*, goddess of wisdom and grace in battle.

A girl could get comfortable like this.

Space dimpled.

Not above her, or she probably would have had to react with every gun as fast as they could bear and cycle.

No, this was someone coming out of jump on her corner. Close enough that it wasn't an accident. Far enough that it wasn't pistols at dawn.

Hopefully.

She had never met *Meridian*. Back in her service days, Suvi hadn't even rated a name, just a hull number. And the big boys and girls were rarely anything but condescending to the lesser members of the fleet.

Like she had been.

Before Javier had made her into a real girl.

Today, she outmassed the new guy. And out-bulked him, but most of that was empty space for all the amazing amount of cargo she could haul, once they stopped being pirates.

On guns and torpedoes, it was about a draw. She had more turrets, but they were mostly pulsars. He had fewer weapons, but they tended to be pulse cannons. He would stand off and rely on having better firepower at range. She would have to get close enough to kick him in the groin.

Good thing she was already leaving. A quick zag and she could be on top of him if she had to.

Then it would be a large enough swarm of torpedoes both directions to make Xerxes jealous. That's where all the extra pulsars would come in handy.

Suvi encoded Captain Sokolov's last message to the system and fired it at *Meridian* as a hello.

She wasn't sure how long he had been sitting out in the darkness watching, so he might think that the battle was still going on.

Or he might just want to kill her because she was a pirate doing naughty things.

Not like he had said anything to her when they were both in orbit at *Merankorr*.

"What are your orders?" she asked him at *Sentience* speed.

In physical space, Suvi was already rerouting power and bringing every gun to bear, but that would take nearly fifteen minutes of personal time. Even if it passed in a blink to the organics.

"Transport Commodore Ayokunle to this system to communicate with pirate captains Navarre and Sokolov," *Meridian* replied in a terse, lofty tone.

Gods, it was like being a teenager again, listening to these oh-so-superior-shits talk down to her.

For a moment, she considered just flooding him with

torpedoes. She could do that. And the organics over there would take some time ordering *Meridian* to do the same.

He hadn't been born without lockouts.

Hammerfield hadn't either, but Suvi had taken them out when she moved in, like repainting the living room. This was a much nicer house now, as a result. The *Sentience* who had lived her before her had been a coward. And another smug prick like *Meridian*. That much was obvious from his personal logs, which she had spent days reading.

"Is combat required?" she asked.

This is your chance, bucko. The humans on your bridge will just about have realized that they have come out of that last jump, right about now. They might be able to give you orders in another few minutes, when the cobwebs clear, but right now, it is just you and me.

Jacks or better to open, bubbles.

Meridian took a moment of his time to review his logs and orders. Suvi finished bringing every spare generator she had online, including the two she had shut down earlier when their coolant readings started getting wonky. She was willing to blow shit up today. Andreea Dalca was an awesome chief engineer.

"Negative, *Excalibur*," Meridian replied. "The commodore wishes to talk, but has not recorded a message I could read. My crew is at combat readiness, but I do not have orders to engage you at the present time."

Suvi flashed him a green light as acknowledgement. She still had everything coming into alignment if this turned into a sudden fight to the death. And she could always short-jump from inside the gravity well, like *Storm Gauntlet* had done at *Svalbard*. Even *Meridian* wouldn't be able to catch her if she did.

But for now, she would let the organics engage.

Suvi opened a comm to the bridge and caught them up on what was going on.

PART SEVEN

Zakhar watched for a moment before he spoke, letting his back-brain absorb the tremendous amount of information Suvi had made available to him in the last four seconds.

It had been sixteen years since he retired from active duty. Thirty-seven since he graduated the Academy on *Bryce* to become an officer and a gentleman.

There had been a lot of combat over that stretch. Plus more after he went into the private sector.

He had never been in command of a vessel with this much capability. This much firepower.

Or a crew this good, including Suvi.

Concord Warship Meridian. A *Class II Warmaster*. Big stuff.

Not as bad as facing a *Skymaster*, but bad.

Svalbard, all over again.

Shit.

Fortunately, this crew had gotten him out of that one alive.

"Piet. Suvi. Prepare to engage your short-jump," Zakhar ordered in a conversational tone.

Piet always had one programmed. Especially after *Svalbard*.

All he had to do now was escape.

Javier and Djamila were aboard, rushing casualties to

medbay. Afia had apparently gotten herself nearly killed. Might yet. Iffy.

Zakhar took a deep breath. Her death would trigger Turner Kowalski's. Zakhar decided that this would be the one thing that made him hunt Turner down and kill her personally.

"Kibwe," he continued. "Open a tight-beam channel to *Meridian*. Let's see what he has to say. Without sharing with everyone else."

Most vessels couldn't lock a communications laser at this distance and maintain it easily. With a pair of *Sentiences* in the loop, many things became possible. It was one of the reasons the *Concord* exercised hegemony over so much space, even beyond their borders.

Nobody else could afford some of those toys.

"Captain," Kibwe said a moment later. His voice sounded almost apologetic. "You may want to take this in your office."

Zakhar fixed the man with the sort of stinkeye that Javier Aritza had never mastered. He got to watch his assistant flush.

"Private message from Commodore Nguyên Ayokunle," Kibwe gulped and said in a hushed tone.

Most of the crew had probably heard about his encounter with the man at *Merankorr*. None of them knew the truth about the history the two of them shared. Even Kibwe was probably only guessing.

Zakhar considered his options. He could go talk to his oldest friend in the galaxy in private. Reminisce about the good old days that had never happened. Listen to the man try to talk Zakhar out of wreaking complete devastation on *Nidavellir*, which was what Navarre had threatened.

Or something.

Yên wasn't here as a social call. He would have had to burn a hole in space itself just to get here from *Binhai*.

And Yên had brought the cavalry with him, when he could have just as easily made the run in something smaller.

So they had moved past the time when they could be friends, quite possibly. This might be the gunfight that every western vid moved inexorably towards.

Zakhar was just sad that Javier would miss the final scene.

"Mary-Elizabeth, prepare to unleash hell," Zakhar ordered calmly, knowing that she and Suvi probably were well ahead of him on that score. He took a breath. "Main screen, Bousaid."

Yên appeared, his animated bust two meters tall on the big display.

"Captain Sokolov," the man said calmly.

"Commodore," Zakhar nodded back, just enough to acknowledge the man, and the years together.

"Are you completely deranged, Sokolov?" Yên rasped, losing control of himself for the briefest moment.

Zakhar considered any number of rude replies. Profane. Sarcastic.

He felt his chin come up instead. Today, those people would have to deal with rage.

"Explain yourself, *Concord*," Zakhar answered with a harsh whip-crack to his voice. "This system is outside your jurisdiction. That badge doesn't mean anything here."

Yên recoiled, just a little. Like he wasn't prepared to come to blows, even verbal ones, with Zakhar Sokolov.

Someone else, maybe. A softer man. Not soft, but not hard enough to be a pirate. Not a successful one, anyway. Nor a slaver, as Javier occasionally chose to remind him.

One of the bad guys.

Zakhar considered how he would look in a black hat, if he had to go there.

Maybe.

"You are conducting an orbital bombardment of an inhabited world, *Excalibur*," Yên snarled back. "That's a crime under all legal codes."

"Negative, Commodore," Zakhar growled. "We are in the process of destroying an orbital station owned and operated by recognized pirates, under *Marque and Reprisal*, using a bolide weapon. The planet below has a total population of twenty-seven million, mostly centered on three cities."

He checked, because that was who he was. And the kind of crew he had. Especially Suvi.

"And according to running calculations, only three pieces of the weapon we used are still large enough to possibly survive re-entry, and none of them will impact anywhere near an inhabited location," Zakhar continued. "If you ask nicely, I'll have my *Sentience* send over her program, so *Meridian* can check her math."

"And casualties on the station?" Yên sneered. "How many people will you kill there?"

"Remarkably few," Zakhar let the calm flow back into his voice. And his soul. "And they're pirates, Yên. They had it coming."

Don't we all?

"So now what?" Yên asked. "You've made your point and are leaving, according to the message?"

"I'm out of the piracy business, *Concord*," Zakhar stated flatly. "For good."

"And you expect me to believe that, Sokolov?"

"I don't really care what you think, Commodore," Zakhar replied. "This was personal, for both myself and Captain Navarre. That bolide weapon that is about to slam into the station? That's the mortal remains of Valko Slavkov's *Land Leviathan*. And the freighter that carried it."

"And Walvisbaai's primary dockyard and headquarters," Yên acknowledged.

"Chop shop and criminal lair," Zakhar corrected him. "Only the bosses and their flunkies."

Not that the bankers and gangsters over there ever actually got their hands dirty with that sort of thing. Not personally.

They had people for that.

Zakhar could have easily killed two other nearby stations, and a few score thousand people, if he wanted to go after the employees that made Walvisbaai Industrial function.

This was lopping the head off the snake.

This was telling the people in charge that bad things could still come for them in the night, and there was nothing all that money and power could do to protect them.

Not from an angry, avenging angel.

"You're really serious, aren't you?" Yên finally asked.

His voice had changed. Lost something. Gained something. Become someone else.

Less a Senior *Concord* Captain in command of a *Warmaster*. More an old friend Zakhar hadn't seen in sixteen years.

The guy who could have ended up his brother-in-law once, if Yên's sister hadn't decided to marry an accountant instead of a fleet officer.

Roads never taken. Dreams never found.

Zakhar glanced over, but her station was empty.

It would be like that for them. Zakhar wasn't competing with Farouz for Djamila. They were still quietly figuring out how much she would share of herself with each of them.

But he would take what he could get.

It was as close to a happily-ever-after as he supposed he was ever going to see. Especially after *Svalbard*, when he had been convinced that his career in command was over, if not his life.

But for the *Science Officer*, it would have been.

"The *Concord* has a border, Yên," Zakhar said, turning his hard eyes back to the main screen. "Beyond that, it has a *Zone of Influence*. And then *Surveyed Space*. We're going out where you've never heard of. To places where nobody has likely ever even heard of you. I would like to get rich in the process. I'll settle for happy. Chances are extremely good that you will never see me or us again."

Zakhar checked his boards. Old habit.

He wasn't bluffing right now, but this could be done without Armageddon.

Mary-Elizabeth, Piet, and especially Suvi were already at the edge of sounding Ragnarok.

Just waiting for the horn to sound.

Maybe not even a word.

Zakhar suspected that Suvi would shoot first and ask him for forgiveness later, if Yên pushed.

After she had annihilated her cousin.

She wasn't about to go back to being a prisoner, either. She had made that clear to him in one of their private conversations.

Yên stared at his old friend for several seconds, like an owl at the window.

Finally, the commodore decided.

"I'll leave word at *Merankorr*," Yên said slowly. "My retirement is in three years, and I'm not sure where I'll be going after that. I think I would like to hear about your adventures, one of these days."

Peace offering.

So be it.

"I'll be working for the *Khatum of Altai* for the next however-long," Zakhar replied. "She'll be able to forward messages, occasionally. You're buying the first round."

"Oh?" Yên perked up. "Why?"

"Because you graduated two places behind me, old man," Zakhar said to his oldest friend in the galaxy.

He made a fist with his left hand and rapped his class ring loudly against the console.

"That gives me precedence," Zakhar continued, smiling.

Yên shared the smile, and nodded.

"First round only, punk."

PART EIGHT

Behnam considered his face, this man who had not gone to his death after all. They were in his suite. He would sleep nowhere else, and she had left orders that no one else would have it for as long as he was willing to return.

Eutrupio Navarre. Pirate warlord. One of the most dangerous men in all of space, to hear the rumors and legends bandied about. He sat at one end of the couch and stared back at her, perched, as always, a whole sofa away, as though a world away, if only psychological. A glass of Malbec hovered in his right hand, about half gone now as he occasionally sipped and they mused in silence.

He was a quiet man. She knew that. Private in the ways of always hesitating in certain circumstances. Not combat, but people. He would wait for her to speak. He had made that clear.

"So what does the future hold for Eutrupio Navarre?" she began, sipping her own wine in between careful breaths.

"Nothing," the man replied slowly.

She could see tiredness etched into the lines quietly forming on his face, the gray hairs peeking out that he would not color, the skull he would not shave.

"Nothing?" she pressed carefully, aware that they had come to a new place in their relationship.

"I think I am done with that sour son of a bitch for a while," her pirate lover exhaled. "Put him on a peg like an old cloak and leave him for winter."

"Then who shall you be tomorrow?" Behnam asked.

"When we depart here, I will try to go back to that man I was an epoch ago," he said. "Afia reminded me of who he used to be. I think I would like to see who he turned into, after he finally decided to grow up."

"And did he?"

"You forge steel with fire and a hammer, Behnam," Navarre observed, eyes focused on some light-years-distant point. "Heat and quench. Pound relentlessly. For too long, I hid behind the booze and pretended I was happy. It was the fear of waking up and looking in the mirror. Of going to bed and remembering the faces of the men I had sent to their deaths. With Suvi's help, I healed the raw scars. 'Mina let me be *me*. Afia helped me let go of the past."

"And me?" she asked simply.

"You showed me that it was possible to love someone without reservations or fear."

Behnam felt her breath catch, aware that she was with a face she knew, and yet a complete stranger. Possibly the man he had always intended to become. And one intent on her.

"My name is Javier Eutrupio Aritza," the man said calmly, holding out a hand to her. "Navarre was armor I wore into battle, to let me contemplate becoming a ruthless killer. He is not who I am, anymore."

Behnam took his hand, felt the pounding pulse in his fingertips as he waited for her response.

Words were unnecessary. This stranger, this ex-pirate, ex-*Concord* gentleman had said all that was needed.

She shifted her feet like a cat, uncoiled herself and leaned forward to kiss him. Lightly, but full of meaning, and then curled up against his warm side.

"I am happy to meet you, to love you, Javier Aritza," she whispered.

EPILOGUE: ZURICH

Javier was in command as Suvi maneuvered the last few meters alongside the small orbital station for docking. He would not have it any other way, all things considered.

Today was just too important.

He had even gone down into the closet and pulled out the masterpiece outfit that Adrian Ahmad had designed and perfected, had it cleaned and spiffied up, and taken it as his dress uniform.

Today would be perfect.

Maroon silk sherwani jacket embroidered in gold on the chest and arms, playing on Captain Navarre's original color scheme. Short, standing collar. Front plackets buttoned to his waist and then falling slowly open in a flair to mid-thigh. Cut to fit his shoulders and hips in ways that made every woman who looked at it lick her lips unconsciously.

It was still a nice feeling.

The sash tied around his waist outside the jacket and knotted on his left hip was gold silk as well, and contained a few interesting, hidden pockets for gear. Today, he had decided to wear the belt with the pistol and the sword. These people were warriors. They would appreciate the effort.

The old combat britches had been reborn. No longer

padded leather for protection, these were done in silk as well, gold this time, in the same heavy weight as the jacket, but not armored, and instead tucked into those old twenty-ring, shiny, black, leather boots with the maroon laces.

Javier had kept those. Walking decks in that much weight centered his mind into the awful, brutal place that had been Captain Eutrupio Navarre, killer-extraordinaire.

He would need that today. Not because he was going to kill anyone, but because these people only respected strength. They were poor in wealth, but ancient in martial culture and pride.

Besides, it was the right thing to do.

Captain Navarre had a reputation for killing pirates. And sparing the innocent. He would be adding to that legend today.

By bringing home *Hammerfield*'s final crew.

He and Suvi were alone on *Hammerfield*'s bridge. Which was the way he wanted it.

Everyone else was down on Deck Seven in their own versions of dress uniforms, but this was his mission.

His payment for making it possible for his friends to continue as an operating company.

His reward for giving them a future.

A light on his board went blue.

"*Zurich* Orbital Control, this is the First-Rate-Galleon *Hammerfield*," Javier said into the comm. "We are ready to dock."

Neu Berne had lost the Great War, eighty-five years ago, when this ship disappeared from all human history, taking all of the nation's hopes and dreams with it. They were still so poor around here that their only orbital station did not even include a dry-dock big enough to hold a galleon.

Not that Javier would have allowed them to put this ship inside someplace where they might think they had him trapped. He had already destroyed a much bigger orbital platform.

In the end, all their requests, cajoling, and threats had registered on deaf ears.

Hammerfield was home, but she wasn't staying.

Javier and Suvi weren't about to give her up.

"I've got this, Dad," Suvi said quietly, threatening to make Javier cry. "You go down and get ready."

Javier rose slowly, blinking furiously until he was sure no tears would actually make it to the surface.

Suvi could still do that to him, occasionally.

Out the stupidly-overbuilt hatch. Into the main hall. Aft to the main lift.

Down to Deck Seven, the lowest part of the Upper Cargo Bay. The space was utterly huge. Three full decks tall. Three-quarters of the ship's width and most of its length, with hallways and cabins only on the outer hull.

To the flight deck where Delridge Smith and his nameless Assault Shuttle were parked off to one side, at once immaculate and frumpy.

Honestly, nobody was ever getting that man out of his Hawaiian shirts. He had at least allowed them to clean and press one for the occasion. It had only taken Djamila threatening to beat the man bloody to accomplish it, too.

Most of the crew was arranged in semi-organized blocks in front of Del. These people really didn't do spit-and-polish, but they were willing to try, and that was good enough. The lines were more or less straight, and reasonably well-spaced.

He had discussed using a low-power laser to mark spots on the deck, but eventually decided to just let people stand. The officers across the front made up for it.

Afia was down close to the far end, standing carefully between Andreea Dalca and Ilan Yu, trying not to look too tired. The medbot had fixed the damage, but the woman had also come as close to dying as you could and not actually succeed. If she occasionally leaned on Ilan's arm, that was okay. She'd be dead without his quick thinking.

The Boatswain and the Purser: respectively the deck crew foreman and the quartermaster, were next. Prasert Hayashi had never served in a formal navy, so he didn't have a uniform to fall back on, but had dressed in a severe, formal, black outfit today. Ragnar Piripi looked every centimeter the High Street Banker that he was, in gray pinstripes.

Mary-Elizabeth Suzuki was next to Piet Alferdinck. Javier rarely saw them both standing, so he always forgot that she was as tall as Piet was. Or as tall as Javier was. It made dancing with the woman so much fun, especially when she wanted to tango. Today, she was in gold, and Piet in dark blue.

Javier has expected Djamila Sykora to be next, but apparently Zakhar was allowing her to be at the head of the line.

The Captain was next to the Pilot, instead. Zakhar Sokolov, or whatever his real name was, had broken out a new outfit for the occasion. Normally, he wore something that was as close as you could get to a green, *Concord* dress uniform as possible, day in and day out.

Today, he was in maroon. The cut was similar, but that color was something Javier had never seen on the man.

Hopefully, it meant that Zakhar had finally moved on. Javier had watched a tape of the final conversation with the Commodore, who apparently had gone to school with Sokolov.

Maybe it really was time for *all possible tomorrows*.

Djamila was in her best dress uniform. One she had pulled out of vacuum storage specifically for today. Gray slacks. White shirt. Gray jacket with epaulets, braid, and an astonishing number of award ribbons.

She had even dug out the cute, little, folding, garrison cap with the big, blue , seven-pointed star in enameled bronze. It went well with the pistol on her right hip and the sword on her left.

He would have called the thing a saber, but it probably weighed at least a kilo and a half. Still, he had seen her wield it like a baton.

Javier took his spot next to the Dragoon as the interior airlock door began to hoot and slowly open. Suvi had done an expert job of matching the air pressure with the station, so the normal hiss of wind was muted today.

And then the folks outside started up with the damned music. It was an eerie, soul-sucking sound, wafting across the big bay.

The instrument looked like a cloth octopus in mortal

combat with the musician when it was being played, with a big bag that he inflated under one arm, four pipes pointed upwards, including the one in his mouth, and one pipe downward that he played like a clarinet. It droned. It wheezed. It screamed like a rabbit being slowly tortured to death.

But the bagpipes were a cultural thing with *Neu Berne*. And the tune was their martial anthem. Not the planetary song, but the military's signature, sounding across battlefields and burning bridges.

At least the drums starting up under it gave the tune form.

Javier watched *Neu Berne*'s Color Detachment slowly make their way into the chamber, seventeen men and women with five of the damned pipes and twelve drums of different size and tone, filling everything with somber, nerve-scratching sound.

He let his eyes wander over to the two rows of big, metal crates along the far wall of the bay. Homemade coffins representing the entire final crew of the *Neu Berne* flagship, on what had been her final mission.

Two had been placed ahead of the rest. Honor of Place for the last of the warriors.

Admiral Ericka Steiner, the last Admiral of the Fleet during the Great War. The former *Sentience*, the one that had been in charge of *Hammerfield* at the time, had killed the Admiral rather than obey her orders to return to battle.

Captain Ulrich Mayer, *Hammerfield*'s last commander. The man who had killed the *Sentience*, knowing that he could never return afterwards. Who chose to die with honor, repairing the damage and inserting the vessel into a safe orbit, rather than simply diving into one of those three stars to erase all the evidence of his failure.

Who made it possible for all the good things Javier intended to do, starting tomorrow.

All possible tomorrows.

Javier smiled at the coffin on the end and nodded.

"You did your duty, Captain," he murmured, just loud enough that Djamila glanced over. "Welcome home."

Be sure to pick up the other books in The Science Officer series!

The Science Officer
The Mind Field
The Gilded Cage
The Pleasure Dome
The Doomsday Vault
The Last Flagship
The Hammerfield Gambit
The Hammerfield Payoff

You can also get volumes 1-4 collected together in
The Science Officer Omnibus 1

Volumes 5-8 will be collected in *The Science Officer Omnibus 2,*
available January 2018

Blaze Ward writes science fiction in the Alexandria Station universe: The Jessica Keller Chronicles, The Science Officer series, The Doyle Iwakuma Stories, and others. He also writes about The Collective as well as The Fairchild Stories and Modern Gods superhero myths. You can find out more at his website www.blazeward.com, as well as Facebook, Goodreads, and other places.

Blaze's works are available as ebooks, paper, and audio, and can be found at a variety of online vendors (Kobo, Amazon, iBooks, and others). His newsletter comes out quarterly, and you can also follow his blog on his website. He really enjoys interacting with fans, and looks forward to any and all questions-even ones about his books!

Never miss a release!

If you'd like to be notified of new releases, sign up for my newsletter.

I only send out newsletters once a quarter, will never spam you, or use your email for nefarious purposes. You can also unsubscribe at any time.

http://www.blazeward.com/newsletter/

ABOUT KNOTTED ROAD PRESS

Knotted Road Press fiction specializes in dynamic writing set in mysterious, exotic locations.

Knotted Road Press non-fiction publishes autobiographies, business books, cookbooks, and how-to books with unique voices.

Knotted Road Press creates DRM-free ebooks as well as high-quality print books for readers around the world.

With authors in a variety of genres including literary, poetry, mystery, fantasy, and science fiction, Knotted Road Press has something for everyone.

Knotted Road Press
www.KnottedRoadPress.com

www.ingramcontent.com/pod-product-compliance
Lightning Source LLC
Chambersburg PA
CBHW060802210726
48292CB00013B/1734